D0200439

BY CHARLIE PRICE

CHARLIE PRICE

DESERT ANGEL

FARRAR STRAUS GIROUX
NEW YORK

To Kit Anderton—friend and brother

Copyright © 2011 by Charlie Price
All rights reserved
Distributed in Canada by D&M Publishers, Inc.
Printed in the United States of America
Designed by Jay Colvin
First edition, 2011
1 3 5 7 9 10 8 6 4 2

macteenbooks.com

Library of Congress Cataloging-in-Publication Data
Price, Charlie.
    Desert Angel / Charlie Price. — 1st ed.
        p. cm.
    Summary: In the California desert, fourteen-year-old Angel is on
the run from the man who abused her, killed her mother, and intends
to kill her too.
    ISBN: 978-0-374-31775-1
    [1. Survival—Fiction. 2. Violence—Fiction. 3. Illegal
aliens—Fiction. 4. Mexican Americans—Fiction. 5. California—
Fiction.] I. Title.

PZ7.P92477Des   2011
[Fic]—dc22

2010044122

1

The fight started after midnight, Scotty drunk, Angel's mother shrill on crystal. When it didn't die down, Angel left the trailer to sleep nearby in a small draw where one of the drainage creases made a cradle. Screened from night winds, cut off from the yelling and threats, Angel could nestle in her robe and watch the stars. She no longer made wishes. Fourteen was too old for wishes. Sleeping outside was just one more thing that had to be done. When she awakened at dawn, the truck was gone and the trailer was empty. The inside wall by the door was bloody.

LATER ANGEL WISHED SHE'D CHANGED CLOTHES, shed her robe and put on jeans and a jacket. Wished she'd grabbed her daypack and taken the bread and a couple of water bottles. But no. She had to find her mother. Couldn't think of anything else.

The pickup tracks went north, away from the westbound dirt ruts that connected their squatter camp to Dillon Road. Maybe she'd noticed that before she went into the trailer. Maybe that caused the rush. Angel knew there was nothing north except cactus and yucca and tall scree ridges that bordered the California desert.

She had walked twenty minutes or more when she stopped to slip off a shoe and shake out an annoying piece of gravel. In that quiet moment she heard the drone of Scotty's truck bucking terrain in compound low and found his line of dust on the horizon. She stepped out of her sweatpants, used them to erase her footprints as she scrabbled several yards from the track to flatten behind a creosote bush.

She waited until he passed before looking up. Seemed like he was alone in the cab. She didn't pay any attention to the brief flood of sadness. Sorrow can make its own desert and Angel's tears dried a long time ago. If anything, she would occasionally notice a knot of anger burning somewhere in her chest. When the truck was out of sight, she stood, shook her pants out, put them on, and resumed walking.

Four months ago, Angel and her mom had been running from a guy named Jerry, another in a long string of abusive boyfriends picked with the accuracy of a heat-seeking missile. They'd hitched out of L.A. heading for Arizona. Supposed to find a cousin in Phoenix. A ride they caught in Ontario let them off at a truck stop in Cabazon. Angel's mom struck up a conversation at the lunch counter while they waited for their burgers. Scotty was an easy acquisition.

Clever Scotty. In the truck stop he told them he was a hunting guide. Wrong. Turned out to be a gun dealer who trapped eagles and tortoises for quick money. He drove them east into the badlands. Big old GMC pickup towing a twenty-foot American Freedom trailer, both painted camo. Past Desert Hot Springs he took some dirt ruts into the flats and stopped at the jagged ridges bordering Joshua Tree. From a distance their camp looked just like more sagebrush. The beatings didn't begin until the third week of the new relationship. Scotty didn't climb in bed with Angel until the fourth week.

FOLLOWING HIS PICKUP TRACKS AND, finally, the drag marks, Angel found her mother's shallow grave before noon. She pawed through the loose dirt until she uncovered a wrist, pulled till she cleared the hand. Her mother's fingernails were broken. Scotty had torn the rings off. Angel pictured her mother clawing at Scotty's eyes. Scotty. Angel had no weapon to kill him. That would have to wait.

Her mother. Lila Lee Dailey. Gone to dust. Angel could feel the cry coming, bad, huge, and it scared her. What if she couldn't stop? What if she broke apart? She pushed the sadness away. Got hold of it. Wadded it up. Made it tiny. Put it down deep. She could bring it back later if she wanted to. Right now there were other things.

Sitting beside the grave, Angel knew she couldn't leave until she fixed it. Piled rocks on it high enough and wide enough to keep the coyotes out. She would roll in the dirt around the mound to mask any blood residue with her scent. She didn't realize she might have learned that from Scotty. But first things first: a good place to hide if he came back.

She scanned the area. A climbing rock? A cave? Nope. A patch of scrub? Too obvious. She would have to dig. Fifty yards farther north, past a mesquite thicket, she scooped a shallow depression behind one of the yucca plants dotting the valley floor. If Scotty returned, he'd see the rock mound over the grave. He'd look for her. Might check nearby bushes, the obvious places, in case his arrival had surprised her, but he wouldn't walk far. He wouldn't guess she'd go to much trouble to hide. He accused her of being silly and lazy. He would figure she'd run. Head west to Dillon Road, to Thousand Palms, maybe on to Cathedral City. Well, she would. Later.

The search for heavy stones required care. Rattlers. Scorpions. An eroded ledge nearby offered some heavy sand clods at the top, several loaf-sized stones along the bottom. It took her a couple of hours to carry them and cover the grave. When she finished she was seriously thirsty. She thought for a moment but found no solution. She collected her robe from the graveside, and used its hem to brush footprints back to her burrow. Nothing else to do but lie down, pull the robe over her, and wait until dark.

2

Her own scream caught her by surprise. Brief but loud. Did she dream it or do it? And then she was listening to an engine. Maybe that's what woke her. She listened harder but could no longer hear over her heartbeat. She resisted the urge to raise her head or do anything to give herself away. Struggling to calm herself, she picked up the sound again, nearer. The engine stopped and a door opened.

RUNNING AND HIDING. She'd gotten pretty good at that. Not much memory of her childhood. Years ago her mom had a job. Gone a lot. Angel stayed with some woman. Dirt backyard but you could see big ships parked in the Bay from the woman's porch. After that, the trucker in Redding. Angel went to school a little bit there. Later, the fat security guard. His house smelled like feet. And the biker. Angel lost track. Up to Jerry. Jerry and the dog collar. Scotty hadn't been any worse than that until last night.

SHE FLINCHED WHEN THE TRUCK STARTED AGAIN but she didn't look until the sound of the engine faded almost out of hearing. If he hadn't hit the brakes for a second, she wouldn't have located him heading west. He thought he might catch her on the move. Angel stood. Dusk. Not enough light for him to see her in the rearview mirror. Plus, he wouldn't be looking. He'd be wondering which way she'd go when she got to Dillon Road. That made up her mind. Back to the trailer. Water and a weapon. She was sure she could find a weapon. She knew as she walked. The best weapon would be a phone.

THE TRAILER STILL BAKED from the late afternoon heat. Inside, she was right. Weapons everywhere. But first water. Her mom always kept a cool quart in the fridge. She drank that down and then a Coke that made her belch so hard her chest hurt. And then another bottle of water. She made herself go slower so she wouldn't get sick. Scanned for a phone. None in sight. Sat at the fold-out kitchen table until her stomach settled.

Okay. She was ready to outfit. She picked up a hunting knife Scotty kept by the sink and carried it to her daypack. First things first. How much time did she have? Fifteen minutes? An hour? She had to disable the trailer. The cops would want to see it. Find the blood. What if she stuck a knife in the sidewall tire? Would it blow up?

Outside at the wheel well she knelt, made a quick study, noticed the valve stem. When she cut it off, air came out in a steady hiss. She did the other three. The trailer settled to its leveling blocks. She located two spares and sliced them. Not going anywhere now.

Back inside, part two of her plan. Protection. She searched the bedroom, found the suitcase full of pistols. Picked a short one with a big hole in the end. How did Scotty load these? A metal holder came out of the handle. How? She pointed it away from her and looked it over. Pushed the small knob at the bottom of the grip. The bullet case slid out and hit the floor. Angel didn't pick it up until she stopped shaking.

Okay. The metal thing was full of bullets. She put it back and carried the gun to the outside doorway. Her legs were unsteady. Hunger? Fear? She took her time setting the pistol on top of the TV, making sure it was stable, making sure it wouldn't fall, before she got more water bottles from the fridge. Drank half of one, took a breath, and finished it. Rummaged in the paper sacks on the counter. Found the bread, jammed a couple of pieces in her mouth, and washed them down. She held on to the counter till she felt solid again.

At the door she lifted the pistol out straight in front of her and pulled the trigger. Nothing happened. Was it broken? Did the drop wreck it? She pictured Scotty ejecting the shell case, checking the bullets, shoving it back, and jacking the barrel. It took her another minute to make the barrel move. Something snicked in place. She held the gun out again and pulled the trigger. The noise deafened her and her hands flew upward as the pistol bucked out of her grasp and hit the top of the doorway before bouncing down the steps into the sand. She followed it, picked it up, and cocked it again. This time a bullet jumped out into the air and fell to the ground. Why was this so complicated?

She was trembling. Running out of time. Back at the suitcase she found a pistol where she could see the bullets in the round cylinder. The end hole wasn't as big but it would probably do. Back at the doorway, it wouldn't fire. She raised it to toss it away, stopped, examined it again. A plastic plug behind the trigger thing, jammed between it and the handle. She pushed it out with a fingernail, aimed outside, and pulled the trigger. Explosion. But this time she held on.

All right for protection. Next, supplies. Jacket, cap, sunglasses, tennies, daypack with water and food. She tore off her sweatpants and pulled on jeans. Last, search out the phone. She hurried. Counters, shelves, drawers? No deal. He must be carrying his and her mom's. She had just given up when the floor jiggled.

Scotty stood in the open door.

"Hi, honey, I missed you."

She opened her mouth but could not speak.

"You did a nice job with the grave. I would have done that later."

Where was the gun? Did she set it down? Put it in her pack?

"Have you ever changed a tire?"

She didn't see the fist coming.

3

When she came to on the couch, everything smelled like gasoline. She struggled to get up but couldn't. Ropes. The living room was dark. Through the open front door a dim glow. Could be the pickup's running lights. She coughed and stifled it. Where was he? Outside? The trailer vibrated again.

"Time to go, sweetie."

Angel pretended to be unconscious.

"You know I'd take you, but you wouldn't stay. Prettier than your mom but hella trouble."

She felt his steps come to the couch. Ducked her chin to minimize the blow, but he didn't hit her. He covered her face with a pillow and lay on it. She got half a breath before he crushed her, and she thrashed like hell but in that second she knew it was foolish. She kept the air she had, kicked for another minute, gave a last struggle, and went limp. She could take tiny, tiny breaths but she didn't know whether he could feel them.

When he took the pillow away she smelled beer. Thank god. It would make him dumber. She could hear him fumbling, the scratch of a lighter, and then the flame was at her nose. She forced herself to accept the burn, knew he was checking for air. He moved the lighter to her cheek. She willed herself to be totally still, wall off the pain, but didn't know how long she could stand it; she was running out of air. A few seconds more, and she felt him back off. A rope loosened. Neck, arms, legs. The pressure ceased and the cord brushed the floor as he coiled it.

"Accident, sweetie. These trailers. Happens all the time. Generator. Spark. Gas."

She heard him walk down the living room into the bedroom, back through into the kitchen. Checking things. At the couch he put his hand on her hip.

No.

He rubbed up along her ribs and over her chest. "Miss you."

She could feel him looking at her. Worse than the burn.

He wheeled and clomped out.

She could hear the lighter rasping outside, and then a *whoosh*. When she opened her eyes, the outside door was filled with flame. The propane tank by the kitchen could blow any minute. That left the bedroom back window.

Would he stay and watch? She didn't think so. He'd jam before anybody investigated.

The heat was making her crazy but she had to find the pack. Water. There, on the floor in front of the TV. The fire beat her to it. She gave up and raced to the bedroom. The window beside the bed was too high to kick out. A bat, a club, anything. The closet wall was smoking but she made herself paw the floor. Cowboy boot. Not heavy enough. Ax? Hammer? Both burning in the kitchen. Crawling away from the closet, she scanned the dresser. Above it on the wall, an antelope head, a mounted four-prong buck. She tore it down and swung it by an antler, breaking the glass and then the metal sill. She pushed out the remaining pieces and scrambled after, tucking her head at the last moment, crashing in the sand and rolling. Then clawing, scrabbling, running, until she was knocked off her feet by the explosion.

Debris rattled around her. She couldn't breathe. She couldn't breathe! And then she could, but the sobbing made it hard to catch up. The sand was warm. Something poked her. At the top of her thigh. A rock. She scooted a few inches sideways. Now, lying on her stomach, it was all soft. Soft. She rested her head on her arms.

4

Angel opened her eyes and levered herself over onto her back. Everything hurt. Most, her nose and cheek from the lighter burns. Touching them made it worse. The arms of her thin jacket were torn and crusted with dried blood. Her jeans damp with dark splotches from cuts. She rose to sitting and turned to the trailer. Smoking, black, it was barely recognizable with the kitchen area missing.

The realization took a few minutes. No one came. No one noticed. Maybe no one would even investigate. And then worse. Her mother was probably gone. Scotty would move the body. Make sure she was never found.

Angel watched the ridgeline stars disappear first, fading into a light gray, and the night sky surrendering inch by inch, the blackness leaching out to the quiet glow before sunrise.

She knew she should be walking. Walking while the air was still cool. Walking before water became the main issue. Instead she lay on her back and decided whether she wanted to keep living.

She'd fought to live. Why? Look around. Hard to say. What exactly would make this life worth living? She was broken, stupid. No. She didn't feel stupid. She just didn't know anything. Homeschooled by her mother. Great. She brushed her eyes.

She knew a few things. "First things first." She'd heard somebody say that. She liked it because it made sense. And she knew other people. Not knew them, but knew how to read them. From a mile away. Knew what they wanted and whether they thought they could get it from her. And maybe she knew one more thing. You can't count on anybody. The only one who'll be there for you is you.

She made an inventory starting with what she wore. Jacket, T-shirt, jeans, underwear, tennies. She felt in her pockets. Small scarf. Piece of emery board. Quarter. Earring. In her watch pocket, a five-dollar bill folded the size of a stamp. Great. What could you do besides laugh?

Really, what did she have? Herself. Nothing. The tears surprised her and the sobs became hiccups. She held her breath, made them stop. She hit the ground with her fist, hit it with both fists. Gave up. Useless. The sun had slipped over the ridge unnoticed. It hit her eyes and hurt.

She gained her feet slowly, letting the different pains stretch into a single dull ache. Water? She walked to the trailer. Any water had evaporated, containers melted. Circling the ruins, she saw nothing that wasn't charred or stinking. At the end of her circuit she kept moving, following ruts now, west toward the snowcapped mountains, west toward the paved road and Cathedral City.

Weeks had passed since Scotty had picked them up at the truck stop. They'd driven east on 10. Before long the signs had said Desert Hot Springs, then Dillon Road. Scotty took that farther east until he slowed and turned left on a jeep trail, northeast toward jagged ridges. Angel had been looking out the passenger window, memorizing, calculating, like she'd done for years. It was natural. Know the neighborhood, remember streets. You might have to run.

Her mom had been straddling the floor shift and flirting. Scotty made her scrunch back long enough to put the truck in compound low gear. Said he didn't want the trailer to bob around and pop off the hitch. Half an hour later he found the flat camp at the foot of cliffs that stretched for miles, crumbly, unclimbable, cut with deep ravines. Scotty had unhitched the trailer and parked the pickup facing out. Angel understood: safe hideaway, quick getaway.

Now, walking in the opposite direction, it would take Angel at least an hour to make it back to the pavement. There she remembered houses scattered along the road, remembered the cinder blocks, patched roofs, junky yards; the rusty half-ton trucks with stock rails.

Angel ignored the baking heat, the shadows of birds flying above her, because something was wrong. It took her another mile or so to catch it. She hadn't brushed her footprints. She looked over her shoulder. Sooner or later Scotty would track her.

"Tortoises, pretty easy. You know their prowl, find their marks, circle till you run into one." At the kitchen table, wearing gloves, rubbing scent on a snare chain, he'd cut his eyes at her, sensing her interest. "Eagles, though, pretty tricky. Guerrilla war. Got to be patient. High ground, rotten deer. Got to pop a net on them soon as they land." He had turned his head to look at her fully. "Those, you got to be willing to wait. Got to cover every detail."

She had seen it in his eyes. Tortoise or bird, her time was coming.

So she knew Scotty would come back, make a last check, but maybe not today. He'd wait to see if anybody was going to sniff around the burn. He'd probably glass the place from a distance. If it was clear, he'd go in and poke through the wreck, looking for her bones. When he didn't find them, he'd come after her.

She glanced at the sky. Sure. Like it was going to rain. No, her tracks would still be there, around the ruins, heading out along the trail. She had a head start so she needed to reach the pavement before he caught up. Then he wouldn't know if she'd gone east or west or hitched. If she had water she'd make it for sure. Without it . . .

She covered her head with her jacket and walked faster.

5

Angel's tongue was swollen, her throat raw. She had fallen a couple of times, had gravel in her palms, grit in her mouth. Reaching the pavement was a relief but it was rough, no easier to walk on than the sand. Though she was dizzy, not sure she was seeing right, it looked like a house in a clump of scrub trees close ahead. She plodded toward it, made it to the porch, caught a toe on the steps, and limped to the door. She leaned against the wall and pushed the screen open.

An old woman sitting on a plastic-covered couch looked up from her sewing. Frowned. Stubbed out her cigarette. *"¡Mijo!"* The screech was like metal on metal.

Angel wasn't sure what to do, what to say. Help? Pretty obvious. She sat on the cool linoleum floor and closed her eyes.

A new pain flashed and roused her. Scotty!

The old woman was poking her with a cane. *"¡Levántase!"*
Angel shielded her face with an arm.

"Up." The woman lifted the cane again.

"Okay. Okay." Angel rolled away and got to her knees.
"Water?" Her voice was raspy. *"¿Agua?"*

The woman shooed her as if an animal had entered the
house by mistake.

"Abuela. Momentito."

Angel turned to the voice from the front door. A boy? An
old man? She couldn't make sense of him.

"Sólo sed." The man continued speaking to the gray-haired
woman as he came inside. *"Agua*, water. *Nada más."* The man,
small, bent, had his hands in front of him, placating the
woman.

Angel watched, uncertain. She made an effort to stand, but
the dizziness returned. She slid a few feet to a large chair and
propped herself against it.

The man gave Angel a nod, took the old woman's elbow,
and whispered something as he walked her back to the couch.

Looking past him, the woman squinted at Angel like the
girl was a demon.

The little man caught the old woman's eye and held up a
single finger. *Wait.*

The woman sighed and picked up her sewing. Found the
threaded needle and fitted a thimble to her finger. The man
went through an open doorway to the next room and returned
shortly with a clay jug of water.

Angel drank till she felt sick, wiped her chin with her arm.

"Thanks," she said. Her mother had shown her Spanish in a Mexican guidebook but she wasn't comfortable trying it.

"You are hurt."

Angel shook her head.

"You are lost?"

Angel glanced at the old woman, who continued mending, giving no sign of listening. What would happen if she told part of it? Would he believe her? Would he call the sheriff? If he didn't, what could he possibly do? Scotty would swat him like a bug.

"Your *carro*?"

Angel closed her eyes.

"You run." The man's voice was soothing. "You wish help?"

Angel had heard that before. Social workers. You couldn't believe anybody.

"You rest. Okay."

Angel looked at the man carefully. He was guessing. But he was speaking her thoughts. What did he want from her?

"Hey, Tío, Abuela. A man is looking for his daughter."

6

Angel turned to see a teenage boy holding the screen open. Thick black hair, khaki work pants, UCLA T-shirt. Clean. Only then did she pick up the sound, the low rumble behind him.

The older man was up immediately, moving toward the door. "Tell him no, *no hemos visto.*"

The young man was looking at Angel.

"*¡Aya, Matteo! ¡Dile!* Tell him! We don't see." The old man reached the threshold and blocked the view outside.

"You don't see what?" Scotty. Somewhere beyond the door.

Angel was on her feet, slipping and scrambling through the doorway to the far room. A kitchen. Small fridge, double-burner hot plate, chipped sink, square table set with clay-colored plates, three chairs. If there was a pantry she didn't see it. No crawl hole to the ceiling. But there was another space. Mudroom. She ran through and flew out the screen door. *No!* She dived back and grabbed it before it slammed.

The rear area had a makeshift corral with a stunted heifer, a few goats, and a pig lying in the dirt at the far end. To one side, a broken coop. To the other, a shed big enough for a stall and a workbench. Scotty would search both. Angel forced herself to keep looking. An outhouse. She'd never fit down the hole. At the edge of the place a dilapidated car sat on rims. The trunk? But he'd check it. She turned back to the house. Propane tank at the corner. Roof? No way up. The water she'd gulped was coming back on her. She wheeled. Corral. She could lie behind the pig.

"Angel, sweetie, time to come home." Close, kitchen at least.

Out of time. A surge of panic brought bitter fluid to the back of her throat. She sprinted for the shed, circled it, and crawled into the corral to lie as close as she could to the pig without disturbing it. She heard the back screen open.

"Well, nice spread." Scotty. Friendly as could be. "Got some good animals there," he said. "We didn't have a chance to get our stock going."

Whoever was with him didn't reply.

"Mind if I see how you did your little barn there? Think I want to do mine the same way."

Angel kept her head down but she could hear the footsteps. She couldn't remember if the stall shed had a window facing the corral. Sounded like Scotty and someone following him went inside the shed for a minute or so and came back out.

"That a Pontiac? I used to have one of those."

She heard him walk past the corral toward the old car, heard it groan when he leaned on it to look in, heard the trunk hinge grind open and the clack when he closed it.

"Good one, huh? They give out, you still hate to let 'em go."

She heard his steps come back toward the corral. Then silence. Somebody's boot creaked.

"Goat milk? Make cheese?"

Whoever was with him remained quiet.

"Well, thanks. Mighty neighborly." He cleared his throat. "You see my daughter, keep her safe. Keeps running away, one of these times she's gonna get hurt. Hitch with some nut. I told you I got a reward for her? A thousand dollars. You or your family find her and it's yours."

Maybe whoever was with Scotty nodded. She heard steps receding but not the sound of the screen. They could be walking around the house to the drive. She stayed put till she heard the faint engine noise, heard it move away, heard it speed up and go through gears heading west toward Hot Springs.

The pig shivered and snorted, dreaming, Angel thought. She rubbed the bristly skin along its shoulder and back. Felt like kissing it thanks. Shook her head. The princess and the pig. She carefully rolled away, scooched under the lowest corral rail, and stood. The yard was smaller than she remembered. All dirt. And in the middle boot prints going in different directions and her size-six tennie marks in a ragged line from the rear door toward the back of the shed. Her tracks. The bolt of fear was like a seizure, spewing water and bile up from her stomach into the dirt at her feet.

Angel was bent over, hands on knees, hoping to ease the burning in her throat when she heard the screen door. Abuela. Standing in the opening, watching. The old woman used her cane to negotiate the step, came forward holding a wet dish towel. She washed Angel's face and walked her back inside.

7

Matteo leaned against the sink, shaking his head and frowning while Angel sat at the kitchen table with Tío and Abuela. Tío rubbed his hand through his hair. Angel kept her head bowed, but her knee had started jittering and she stuck her hands under the table to hide picking at her hangnails. Abuela was looking at her so intently Angel could feel her skin growing warmer.

The old woman had started with the short blond hair, matted and singed. Angel stopped herself from reaching up to comb it with her fingers. Abuela tilted slightly to better see the cuts on Angel's forehead, the reddened burns on cheek and nostril. She took in the stains on Angel's torn jacket before returning to Angel's face. She focused on Angel's eyes and read them like tea leaves.

"Why didn't you tell him?" Matteo challenged. "Her father. It's her family to work out."

Tío shook his head.

"You're always telling me *la familia es todo*. We can't do nothing with her," Matteo insisted.

Abuela silenced him with a look.

Matteo lowered his eyes, rubbed the instep of one boot against the back of his other leg.

"Not father," Abuela said. *"Son differentes."*

"He's not my father," Angel said, speaking for the first time since Scotty left.

Tío turned to her. Spoke softly but firmly. "You run from him. Okay. He is gone. After dark, you go. No police," he said. "We . . ." He looked away to find the right words. Gave up. Tapped the table for emphasis. "No police here."

"¿Piensas que él lo sepa?" the grandmother asked Angel.

"I don't understand."

"You think he knows?" Matteo translated impatiently. "Knows what? *¿Que?*"

"That I'm here?" Angel didn't need to think. She nodded, not meeting anyone's eyes. "I know he does." In the following silence she wasn't sure they believed her. "He's a hunter." She spoke slowly and looked at Abuela, hoping to be understood.

"Un cazador," Tío translated.

Abuela closed her eyes and crossed herself.

MATTEO PULLED A STOOL OUT OF THE MUDROOM and joined them at the table. Time to make a plan. The family waited, everyone looking down at the place where the plate would be if this were a meal. It was on Angel to speak first.

What could she say? She wasn't used to talking. At all. To anyone. Her mother had told her a hundred times. *Don't say nothing. What we do is nobody's business.* So maybe she could keep them out of it.

"Do you have a phone?"

Matteo snorted. Tío shook his head.

Okay. There was really no choice. Scotty was out there. Watching. If she left, he'd take her. But if she stayed . . . he could torch this place. Or sneak in and— Angel stopped herself, couldn't stand to imagine what Scotty might do to this family.

"I have to go." Angel kept her voice steady, but her eyes were busy searching the kitchen counters for a weapon. Would they give her a knife?

"I'll walk her to Ramón's," Matteo said. "He can drop her at the police on his way to work."

"Walk her . . . ?" Tío was frowning at the idea.

"Okay, I'll wait till Celina comes home and drive her to Ramón's."

"Celina?" Angel asked.

"My sister," Matteo said, sounding irritated at having to explain. "Works in town."

"The man watches?" Tío asked.

"This house?" Angel nodded.

"*¿Él hizo esto?*" Abuela asked. "Man, did? All?" She was pointing at Angel's wounds.

"Yes," Angel said. A surge of shame rushed through her.

Her fault. She should have seen this coming. Should have done something. Made her mom leave. Killed Scotty in his sleep. Run—

Tío interrupted her thoughts. "He will hurt everyone?" he asked, moving his eyes to include Matteo and Abuela.

"Yes," Angel said, swallowing back tears.

Tío stood and left the room. Came back with a small rifle and put it on the floor next to him as he sat.

Angel pitied him. Next to Scotty's high-powered rifles with scopes, Tío's gun was a toy.

Matteo's eyes had widened. "So I'll get her out of here," he said, pushing up from the table. "Out the back. Off the road. Be at Ramón's in fifteen minutes."

"And if Ramón's not home?" Tío was shaking his head. "If this man sees you and does something? . . . Sit."

"*La iglesia,*" Abuela said. "Church. All."

Matteo snorted again. Angel grimaced. It was too late for church years ago. Tío narrowed his eyes at Abuela, as if that would help him see what she was thinking.

"Church," Abuela repeated. *"Tan pronto a que vuelve Celina."*

Angel looked to Tío.

"Soon Celina come, we all go to church," he said, picking up the rifle and standing.

8

When the elderly Ford sedan rattled into the drive, Abuela hobbled out the front door followed by Tío, then Angel, then Matteo. Tío carried the rifle inconspicuously at his side. The young woman driving looked surprised and started to open her door, but Abuela shook her head, made her way to the passenger side, and climbed in front. Tío opened the rear door and crawled in first. Angel and Matteo followed.

"Church," Tío said. *"A la iglesia, ahorita."*

"What . . . who—"

"¡Ándale, Celina! Now!"

While the car rolled back onto Dillon Road, the passengers scanned both directions looking for the camo pickup. The two-lane and the surrounding desert flats appeared empty. They missed the vehicle tucked behind mesquite three hundred yards west, missed the brief glint of raised binoculars.

WHILE CELINA DROVE TOWARD HOT SPRINGS, Angel looked for landmarks in case she had to flee the car. *Right.* The desert flats were crisscrossed by hundreds of identical shallow washes cut by runoff from the rare thunderstorms. Houses were farther apart than she remembered. There were no stores, no businesses, and the miles sped by with numbing sameness.

CHURCH. This was the old woman's idea of a plan? Angel only went along because she thought there might be a phone to call police or a chance to run again without Scotty seeing her. Angel had never given religion much thought, but it wasn't like God or prayer had ever helped anything. If there was a god, he was for other people. Scotty was an ugly man. Maybe worse, but similar to several men her mom had hooked up with. Not the devil. There was nothing supernatural in Angel's world. Nothing was to blame for her mother's death but persistent stupidity. Angel tried to stay with her anger but she missed her mom with an ache that not even rage could cover. She coughed to stifle an involuntary sob.

After several minutes Celina made a right on a dirt road at the edge of town and skirted the settlement until she reached a whitewashed adobe building with a square steeple. In front, a weathered wooden sign said SANTUARIO DE LA VIRGEN DE GUADALUPE. The gravel parking lot was full of dusty cars and dented pickups. Angel could see families climbing the short steps to an open front door, the older women in dark dresses and shawls, the men in white shirts with cowboy hats or baseball caps.

Abuela drew a scarf out of her bag, put it on, and handed one to Celina. Tío and Matteo wore button shirts and straw hats. Though her jeans would blend in, Angel had nothing large enough to cover her short blond hair. She hated to stand out in a crowd but this was such a dumb idea anyway, it could hardly get any worse.

Once inside she followed Tío to a rough pew in a row near the back, far from the altar. Abuela stayed at the door talking with Celina and several other women. A middle-aged man in a black shirt and white collar stood by the pulpit talking with a young couple holding a baby. Angel closed her eyes and listened to the soft buzz of conversation in the room. Sanctuary. She took a deep breath and enjoyed a rare moment of safety. Scotty would never come in here.

She must have dozed. When someone jostled her awake, she saw the priest and the young couple had now been joined by four gray-haired people. She imagined they were discussing a thing for the baby, a christening, probably. Jostled again, she turned to find Abuela shaking her shoulder.

"Put. *Esta camisa*." The old woman held out a large white snap-button cowboy shirt. A stocky square-faced man standing in a T-shirt beside Abuela looked like he might have just taken it off.

Angel looked at Abuela to see if she meant it. The old woman poked the shirt at her again and the stocky man nodded. Angel felt a wave of dizziness. This was crazy. Did she have to wear white for this church or were they giving her clothes like she was a homeless person? Angel didn't want a scene. She began to take off her jacket.

Abuela stopped her. "No . . . *encima.*"

"Over," the man said. "Leave your jacket."

Angel gave up trying to make sense of this and pulled on the garment. Like wearing a sheet. She rolled the sleeves up to hand level.

A boy came up behind Abuela and handed her some khaki pants.

Abuela reached them to Angel. *"Pantalones."*

Angel couldn't believe what she was hearing. She braced against the idea and looked around to see who was watching. Though she was in a crowd, everyone including Tío and Matteo was staring straight ahead. What the—

"Ahorita. Now!" Abuela's face was grim as she pushed the khakis at the girl.

Was this a punishment? Angel fought an impulse to run. She glanced at the front door and noticed Tío and Matteo had moved and were now walking down the center aisle toward the front. Their hats, which they'd left behind on the pew beside Angel, were quickly picked up and carried away by the young man who'd delivered the pants. Angel watched as Tío chose a pew down front, sat next to an older man, and began taking off his shirt. She looked for Matteo but couldn't spot him. *Changing clothes.* She finally got it.

After she'd tugged the pants over her jeans, Abuela held out her hand.

"*Zapatos.*"

Angel thought she understood. "Shoes?"

Abuela nodded and handed her some black cowboy boots that looked two or three sizes too large.

"Over?" Angel asked.

Abuela shook her head.

While Angel slipped off the tennies, the young man returned, bringing Abuela a bright turquoise T-shirt and navy blue slacks. The old woman took the clothes and handed him the shoes Angel had taken off. "Panama," she told the boy.

"*¿Qué?*"

"*Sombrero,*" Abuela said, pointing at Angel and shooing him away.

Angel looked for Celina but couldn't find her. Abuela walked to the back of the church to change. The young man brought the straw cowboy hat and offered it to Angel. When she put it on she smiled in spite of herself. If she kept the brim tilted down, from a distance she would look like a short, heavy Mexican rancher.

Abuela didn't return, and Angel sat beside the stocky older man who had donned a black sport coat that was too small to button. In a way, it made him look younger. The short-brimmed Stetson he'd worn earlier was missing. Angel wondered if he'd given it to Matteo. Someone tapped Angel on the back. She froze.

"When it's over, you go with him." Celina's voice.

Angel quarter turned. Now Celina had a dark red denim jacket over a brown skirt, a matching bandanna tied around her hair.

"Him," Celina repeated, nodding toward the stocky man. "Ramón. He take you away."

"Okay," Angel said. "Thanks." But when she turned around again, Celina was gone. Was that Abuela standing at the back in a baseball cap?

At the end of the brief service, Ramón took Angel's arm and put it through the arm of a plump woman in a dark shawl. "Together," he said, and took the woman's other arm. The three of them walked out with the crowd and made their way to a maroon crew-cab with livestock rails. "Get in back."

Angel had kept her head down the entire walk, but once inside she scanned the parking lot. Scotty's pickup sat just inside the entrance, facing the line of departing traffic. He could see each car.

"Get on the floor," Ramón told her.

No way Scotty could keep track of everyone leaving the church and know how many people were in each vehicle. He wouldn't be able to recognize Abuela's family dressed differently. But the car? Before she knelt she looked at Celina's Ford. It was empty, by itself now, at the far side of the lot. No one was walking toward it.

9

Ramón's house was on a paved lane heading south off Dillon Road, not far from Abuela's. It sat in a thin grove of trees and ocotillo among different smaller cactus that made a garden of sorts. A climbing rose followed a trellis over the front door. The outside wood was painted a celery green and the door and windows were trimmed in white. A home. A real home. Angel couldn't stop looking.

"Stay in till I check," Ramón told her, walking around the truck to help the plump woman get down from the cab.

The woman had been smiling on the walk out of the church. Now her forehead was creased, mouth set. *"¿La pistola?"* she asked him.

"Don't worry, *cara*. I'm just going to the mailbox. See what I see."

The woman glanced at Angel, before going inside.

Angel imagined they must all hate her for bringing this trouble. They could get hurt, and if some of their people were here illegally, they couldn't afford to have police nosing around for any reason. Well, she was sorry. She was nothing but trouble.

When he returned, Ramón was serious but not unfriendly. He opened her door and gave her a hand out. "Looks clear," he said, sweeping the area to the northwest. "I was him, I'd probably search *la iglesia*, then cruise Dillon to see if somebody let you out. After that, whatever. He don't want *policía*, right?"

For the first time Angel wanted to tell. *He killed my mom.* But then what? What could this man do? Telling would just drag him in deeper. His wife would hate that. "No," she said. "You saw him there in the camo truck?"

Ramón nodded.

"He's kind of outside the law. In lots of ways. And . . . he's mean. And dangerous. Really dangerous."

Ramón held the front door for her. When she stopped inside the entry hall, he led her into a shadowy living room. Old-fashioned furniture, mostly dark green, cushy, matching couch and big chair with one of those things you put your feet on. Old-timey lamps turned down dim, a low table, and some other soft chairs like the fancy ones at Salvation Army.

His wife walked in with a pitcher of gray stuff, looked like lemonade. Said, "Sit."

It had lemon in it but it was different somehow, sweet, tangy, and Angel felt like she could drink a gallon without stopping. She made herself put down her nearly empty glass. She wanted to take off the oversized shirt and pants but knew she would feel weird doing that in front of them.

His wife seemed to sense what she was thinking. "Bathroom's in there," she said, pointing to a hall.

Angel got up and left, came back barefoot carrying the borrowed clothes. "Tonight if you could take me to the bus station I'll get out of your hair," she said. "You don't want to get mixed up with Scotty."

"I was him, I'd have an eye on the bus station," Ramón said.

His wife glared at him, like, *Let her go.*

"He can't be everywhere," Angel said.

"He smart, though, right?"

Angel nodded.

"So what's he gonna do? After cruising around hoping to get lucky."

Angel knew but she didn't want to say.

Ramón looked at her. Steady.

Reminded her of the way Abuela looked at her.

"So he'd go back to the Gomez place? . . . Make them talk?"

Angel nodded.

"Good thing they ain't going to be there." He got up from the big chair. "Reminds me. I got to call Hector. Get him to water their stock."

"Let me use your phone." Angel was up and walking toward him.

"No." Ramón's wife. "No phone."

"She's right, uh, what's your name?"

"Angel, but I won't tell them about you or the Gomas family. I'll have them meet me on the road."

"Gomez, but you use this phone, 9-1-1, they come here. That's the way it works. They track the caller. Always. We don't want blues around here asking questions. Don't want INS checking people that help us." He turned back to the phone. "Sit for a minute, let me do the animals and then we'll figure this out."

Ramón's wife had gone back to the kitchen. Angel could hear pots or skillets clank and silverware rattle. Her stomach growled.

Ramón returned and pulled the ottoman close to her chair. "Bus station's a bad idea."

"So take me to the police."

"I could take you close by. Drop you off. But I don't know that that's so good. You got to think it through."

Angel hadn't thought it through. Hadn't thought anything through. She just ran and hid. That's what she was good at.

"Do it. I'll go help Carmen. Be back in a couple of minutes."

Angel was a little stunned. No grown-up had ever told her to think.

THE WALLS HAD PICTURES. A photograph of Ramón younger and thinner, in a uniform. A painting of a tall black mountain rising out of a desert plain. Over the serving board, a photo of cactus blooming. There were shelves with books and plates standing up so you could see colored drawings on them . . . She made herself stop.

Okay, go to the police and they ask her about Scotty and she tells them he killed her mom last night. Was it last night? No, two nights ago. And buried her. Angel can show them where, but he's probably moved her by now. And she tells them he captures turtles and eagles and sells guns. And Angel describes his truck and they get a guy to draw Scotty from her description. And she takes them to the trailer and they go after him. So what's there to think . . . oh. What would they do with her? Where would she wind up? Juvie? Foster care?

She'd been in foster homes. Both of the times her mom had gone to rehab and once when her mom served sixty days for soliciting. The first place had been run by a twisted family who tried to make each kid take psych meds so they could get more money from the court. Another, the family's own son, a ganged-up sixteen-year-old, kept hitting on her whenever they were alone. The third, the Millers, were nice enough, but eleven kids in a three-bedroom house made a zoo.

She'd spent a couple of nights in juvie when she'd run away and wouldn't tell the police her name or where she was staying. That was scary. Neither the guards nor the other girls would leave her alone. And what if this time the foster father was another man like Jerry or Scotty. She couldn't face it. She held her fists to her eyes to keep tears back.

10

The smell of roast meat made her light-headed. Her stomach twisted and she tried not to be sick. She walked to the front porch for some air.

"Hey. You hungry? *Cena.* Dinner. Come eat and then we'll figure this out." Ramón had put on another shirt, light blue, short-sleeve, again with the snaps. Made Angel wonder: was it just style or was there a purpose to it?

She followed him in through the living room and watched him sit at the head of a dark wooden table covered with steaming dishes of rice, and beans, and chunks of a green-gray vegetable she couldn't identify. There was a mound of meat on a platter in the center, and to its side, a small bowl of shredded white cheese, a heavy tripod bowl of salsa, and a round basket covered with a thick cloth napkin. Tortillas?

"You like carnitas, right?" Ramón smiled and tucked his napkin in the neck of his shirt.

"Uh, I don't know," she said, feeling a small edge of queasiness return. Angel had no idea where she was supposed to sit. Where was his wife? And had she ever seen so much hot food at a table? That somebody actually cooked?

"Why don't you sit here," Ramón said, patting a place on his right, "and Carmen will be in with the *limón*. You liked it, right? Lime and pineapple? Better than Pepsi!"

His wife came in shortly carrying two icy pitchers of the lemon drink. When she was seated, Ramón closed his eyes, clasped his hands, and said a brief prayer of thanks, before passing Angel the basket of tortillas. The beans followed, then the meat, and so on till her plate was impossibly full. *"Muy rico,"* he said, smiling and pointing to the food. He and his wife both dug into their plates and began to eat without conversation.

AFTER DINNER Angel's stomach felt like a watermelon. She hoped she hadn't overdone it.

Ramón had cleared the table with Carmen after telling Angel to wait for them in the living room. In minutes both of them were seated on the couch across from Angel. "So, *qué pasa?*" Ramon said. "What have you been thinking?"

Angel was distracted by his wife. She sat a foot away from Ramón, hands clasped over one knee. She had not looked at Angel but her face wasn't angry or condemning or any of the things Angel would expect. Her face was calm, as if this difficulty was one more in a life of many. One more situation to

41

deal with and be done. The woman was beautiful in a way, like the statue of the Virgin that Angel had seen in the church. Beautiful and strong like Abuela. These women were nothing like her mother, who had been thin and pretty in spite of the broken nose that never healed straight. Her mother, all need and drama.

Ramón interrupted her thoughts. "You have family?"

Angel shook her head.

"Nobody? Nowhere?"

Angel looked at the floor. She really was an alien.

"So, what you want to do?"

"Go. Leave. Somewhere he'll never find me."

Carmen looked at her then. As if she was imagining what it would be like to be chased by someone awful.

"No police?" he asked.

"I guess . . . uh, not yet, maybe."

"I been thinking," Ramón said, rubbing the mark his hat made on the side of his head. "Me and friends. We could make a bunch of calls. Pay phones. We could—"

"You can't," his wife interrupted.

"No, listen. She tells me where it happen, a bunch of us report it. Sheriff has to check it out."

Angel remembered the grave. The trailer. No way Scotty could get rid of all the evidence.

"It was just a dirt track," she said. "The first one that goes left, down from Abuela's."

"Past the Gomez house, left toward the hills, toward Joshua Tree?"

42

"Yeah, at the edge—"

The phone rang and Ramón left to answer. When he came back, his face was dark and his hands were fists.

"All the stock. Your truck guy. Must have just missed him. Shot everything. Cow, pig. Hector says they all bled out in the corral. He's not sure what to do."

Carmen had bowed her head and covered her mouth with her hand as Ramón spoke, but now she turned to him. "Tell him to save meat and bury the rest. Tonight. Before somebody sees, tells *la policía*."

Ramón nodded. Left to make another phone call.

When he came back, Carmen had been thinking. "I'm gonna call the padre," she told him. "Get the phone tree going. Tell everybody watch out."

Ramón touched her arm as she stood and watched her as she left the room. He sat heavily, made the couch groan.

Angel studied him. Forty or fifty. She wasn't good with older people's ages. His short sleeves showed thick arms, rough hands. Maybe he was a little fat but mostly he looked solid. Like he could lift a car. His face was lined, weathered, with slabbed cheekbones and strong jaw. If his eyes hadn't been kind, he'd have looked almost scary.

"You're gonna need a good plan," he said. "Can't make no mistake with this guy."

BOTH SAT WITH THEIR OWN THOUGHTS several minutes before Angel spoke. "You could drop me in Thousand Palms or Cathedral City. I could hitch someplace. Arizona, maybe."

"Where?"

"I don't know. Anywhere."

"This guy, what's his name, he got friends?"

"Scotty. I don't know. I think so. Maybe not friends but people who buy from him, people he sells to. He knows this area pretty well."

"So he might have *conocidos*, partners, watching out. You got to get some distance."

"I could work. Get a job."

"You got skills? Experience? You got a Social card? How old are you?" Disbelief on his face. "Somebody gonna hire a kid? By herself? How you gonna even get a room?"

"I could waitress."

"You ever done that? Any job?"

Angel shook her head. Looked at her torn jacket and jeans. "I could do it. I just have to get some clothes."

"Hell, girl, clothes are the *least* of your problems."

In the silence that followed that remark, Angel remembered her inventory back at the trailer. Earring, five-dollar bill. Right. No serious money. No clothes. No skills. She didn't even have shoes anymore. She had nothing worth nothing. Time to give up. But she didn't think Scotty would kill her fast this time. He'd act out on her. She couldn't face it. More foster care? She couldn't face that either. She struggled not to break in front of Ramón.

After a minute he spoke again. "System could probably help. The cops protect you. Hook you up to services. Find you a place to stay. Go back to school."

Angel shook her head. There wasn't any help. Ever. She bit her lip. Can't think like that.

"So what you gonna do?" he asked her.

Die, she thought, and this time she couldn't hold back. Through a haze of tears she could see Ramón, sitting, hands clasped, watching her, but he didn't get up or touch her. She was grateful for that.

WHEN CARMEN CAME BACK TO THE COUCH, she looked tired. "Celina's *carro*. He burned it."

Ramón looked at her. Didn't speak.

"Right at the church. In the lot. Nobody saw till the gas *explotó*."

"Blew up? Catch anything else?"

She shook her head. "Padre said, just the car."

"Huh." Ramón put his arm around his wife. "Maybe we all gotta get some rest," he said, looking at Angel. His eyes narrowed. "No. If we rest, you run, right?"

Angel avoided his eyes.

"Okay, so let's figure this out."

Ramón settled in again with Carmen and each of them folded their hands in their laps and waited for Angel to speak.

In spite of how bad it was, Angel smiled to herself. Good luck being told what to do by these people. Tío, Abuela, Ramón . . . they were always waiting for *her* to talk. Pretty different. Every day her mom had asked Angel what she should do, and every time she would start talking again before Angel had a chance to answer. And she didn't even notice. Her mom would talk about herself 24/7 unless a man told her to shut up. So why did Angel keep missing her so much?

"I need to get away. Out of this area. That's the thing . . . the only thing." Angel was staring at the bookshelves, thinking. "Arizona was a stupid idea. I don't know anybody there. Really, I don't know anybody anywhere, so any place away from here will do."

"Momo up here, or has he gone back already?" Ramón asked his wife.

She shrugged.

"What do you think? He could take her to Rita's place on his way to Brawley."

"Momo? Brawley?" Not names Angel had heard before.

"My brother's son," Ramón said. "Works at the sugar refinery in Brawley. That's about thirty miles south of Salt Shores where Rita lives. He could swing you by on the way, if he hasn't gone already."

"You gonna bring him into it?" Carmen was frowning.

"Hey, we all aren't into it?" Ramón asked her. "You got a better idea, say it."

"*Nuestro sobrino.* What if he gets hurt."

"All I'm saying, *cara*, is everybody is somebody's nephew. Who would you have me put in danger?"

Carmen sighed, but stayed silent.

"Momo's a good boy," Ramón said. "Smart, *listo.* He'll watch out. Take good care of you. And Rita's tough. Got three or four kids, works Head Start. Gotta be tough." Ramón continued to look at Carmen as he spoke, sensitive to her approval.

Carmen was shaking her head. "You said it yourself. What's Rita gonna do with another kid?"

"She got resources, *cara*."

"*Tú sabes*, Ray. They're *pobres*. Poor as mice."

The conversation was a little hard to follow but Angel got the gist of it. She would be a burden, no matter who she wound up with. If she could just get a ride she could go it alone.

"So, yeah," she said, interrupting them. "I'll go with Momo."

11

Angel was on the porch with Ramón and Carmen early the next morning when their nephew drove into the dirt compound. His shiny charcoal-colored pickup raised dust that glinted in the sunlight and added a flint smell to the sweet climbing roses. Angel carried one of Carmen's old sweaters and wore her own freshly washed T-shirt over the woman's green denim jeans that were four or five sizes too large. A woven belt kept them in place. On her feet, a pair of Carmen's tennies, too wide but laced tight enough to work. Ramón had given her a cotton feed-store cap. The lumpy clothes embarrassed her but they were clean and she was grateful. If Scotty drove by he wouldn't recognize her unless he studied her face.

And now a dark-haired, dark-eyed teen in a cowboy hat

was resting his elbow on his open pickup window and giving her a once-over while she looked totally doofus. Great. She took her eyes off his brown arm and gave Carmen a quick hug. She looked at Ramón. Would she ever be able to hug a man without thinking of Jerry or Scotty? She couldn't reach out but she appreciated him more than she could say.

"I get it," he said, smiling. "Hey, good luck. We'll come visit when things die down here a little. Me and some guys are making those phone calls this morning. See what happens." He extended his hand.

Angel shook it.

"Gotta go," Momo yelled behind her.

It wasn't like she had bags. She jogged to the truck and got in. The cab smelled like french fries and fresh laundry. Mexican accordion music played on the radio.

Momo waved and rolled out, taking the lane down Thousand Palms Canyon and over to Highway 10. He drove the speed limit, occasionally glancing at her and fiddling with a toothpick. After he made the turn on 86 South he told her it would take about half an hour, forty-five minutes, depending on the traffic. He smiled. Dropped it. "Heard you had some trouble," he said, keeping his eyes on the road.

Angel had been trying to study him without being obvious. Western shirt, sleeves rolled high, stained Levi's, round-toed boots. His teeth flashed when he smiled. His hands were scraped, his knuckles large like Scotty's, like they'd been broken.

He saw her looking. "Sugar mill. Machinery's tough on hands, but I still got all my fingers. Not all the *hermanos* can say that."

"I don't really speak much Spanish." She kept her eyes forward.

"You'll learn. Pretty interchangeable down here. Used to be Mexico."

Angel hadn't known that but she didn't say anything.

"*Hermano*, brother. *Hermana*, sister," he explained. "Stuff ends in 'a' is usually feminine."

Feminine? Can words be a sex? Thinking that made her blush even though it wasn't what she meant.

"You'll like Rita."

Angel didn't have anything to say to that. She didn't plan to be there long.

"You in school?"

Angel shook her head.

"Me neither. Had to drop and go to work after Mom got sick. Don't matter. I'll get my G.E.D. this fall."

"G.E.D.?"

"General school test. You get your diploma if you're not in school. It's easy."

Angel was interested but she didn't want to ask more questions. Didn't want to sound stupid.

"You got brothers or sisters?"

Angel shook her head.

"Lone wolf, huh?"

Angel didn't respond but she thought about it. She didn't

see herself as a lone wolf, but what? A cactus? She snorted a laugh and covered her mouth, embarrassed. Better to look out the window. Nothing good could come of talking and she wasn't comfortable alone with him in the truck.

She was frustrated to see so much dry open country with no towns of any size. It wouldn't be like she could walk into an urban maze and lose herself. There was enough traffic to make hitching easy, but Scotty might be traveling these roads on the lookout for her. She didn't think he'd give up until she was dead. Didn't think he'd go out of state or change anything about the way he operated.

Momo seemed content to drive and listen to the music. He offered her a stick of paper-covered gum but she declined. She could tell he was really curious about what had happened to her but too polite to pry.

Surrounding the road, the desert sand was bleached nearly white, with scatters of tall palms every few miles like orchards of some kind. Oases? From time to time they'd pass trails through isolated patches of dense shrub leading west toward hazy mountains on the horizon. Through the windshield to the left she glimpsed the blue-gray water she'd heard was the Salton Sea. Far in front to the right the earth took on a brownish hue. "What's that?" she asked.

"The Anza-Borrego. Another desert. Lotta people go out there four-wheeling. Real craggy, rough."

She nodded.

"I work south of that. Brawley. Way greener. Irrigated . . . Oops. Almost missed it."

He turned left onto a narrow paved road beside a StopShop convenience store, and entered a dilapidated residential area in the middle of nowhere. Weathered pastel houses hardly bigger than one-car garages, shabby trailers with tattered awnings, clumps of weeds crowding every mailbox, plastic bags snared against metal fences.

Aside from the strip next to the highway, there was no sign of regular businesses or children playing. Telephone lines formed cross patterns overhead, and above the roofs Angel could see tops of palm trees sticking up like silly green hair. A half-mile distant, lines of trailers faced the giant salt lake under a washed-out sky. A ghost town baking in acres of grit.

"Amazing place, huh?" Momo said, smiling. "Except for the club and the convenience store, people don't go out much. Early morning, dusk, you see kids biking around, guys working on cars in their yard. Sunday evenings a lot of families go to mass down there." He pointed ahead at a light brown metal building the size of two trailers sitting in a graded field near the street.

Angel had trouble believing people lived in these places. They looked abandoned. "Club?"

"There's a marina has a little general store, tables and a counter, sells beer. Like the community center. 'The club' to locals."

Angel felt the hair on her neck rise. She couldn't stay here. She'd stick out. The newcomer. Within two days everyone would know who she was, would know her story. If Scotty got this far, one question would find her.

"The guy's after you, he'd never look here," Momo said, maybe sensing her alarm. "Who would? Right? And Rita's good people. Head Start's a couple of streets over. And you got your choice of houses, see?" He nodded to a deserted wood-shingle cottage, paint faded and peeling, front door standing open, overturned couch visible inside, attached garage open with tires and trash left to rot on the concrete floor.

Momo turned left on a white gravel street of similar houses. In front of the first: a jeep up on blocks, wheels missing. He slowed at the end of the block and stopped at a faded yellow prefab with an old Toyota in the drive. Across the street sat a huge red eighteen-wheeler with a long silver trailer.

"Looks like Vincente's home," Momo said as he parked. "That's his rig. He's like Rita's husband."

Angel started to get out but hesitated when she noticed Momo hadn't moved.

"Let 'em know we're here," he said, opening his cell phone. "They got kids. Maybe they're busy." He blushed, probably unsure how Angel would take his remark. "I mean it's still early. Don't want to wake them up."

Angel realized that she had better pay more attention. She didn't have any experience with these kinds of relationships.

ANGEL HAD PICTURED RITA LOOKING LIKE CARMEN. Plump, short arms and legs, thick brown hair with a home perm. She was way off. The man who introduced himself at the door, Vincente, looked like that, except his hair was naturally curly. He smiled and gave Momo a big hug.

"*Órale*, boy, what's that *vato* been feeding you? Hay? You growing like corn, every time I see you."

"It's my job, Uncle. They beefing me up so they don't need no forklift."

Vincente stepped back and looked at Angel. "You gonna stay with us awhile?" he asked, bowing slightly. "So you're welcome here, in spite of the company you keep," he said, nodding at Momo.

"Invite the girl in, Tonto. Show you got some manners." The woman's voice was followed by a tall, slender, middle-aged Latina striding in from an adjoining room. From a distance, Angel would have thought her a man. Blue jeans outlined long legs, slim hips, a sleeveless Western blouse showed ropy muscular arms. She had a narrow face with thick dark eyebrows. Big smile. "Neither these guys know what to do around a woman," she said to Angel. "Hi, I'm Rita."

Angel, off guard, was speechless.

"You got things? . . . No, of course not. I talked to Ray and Carmen. So you want to wash up, bathroom's down the hall, got you a bed on the porch, private 'cept for the nosy herd of goats that tear this place up when they're not in school. If they bother you, swat 'em."

Angel was still tongue-tied. Too much, too fast, Rita's good-humored confidence was dazzling.

"Go make yourself useful. Finish getting the truck ready," Rita told Vincente, shooing him and Momo from the room. She turned back to Angel and took a deep breath. "Too many changes?" she asked in a softer voice. "Important thing's you're welcome. Take your time. Sit if you want. You hungry?"

Angel shook her head, realizing at the same moment that she was.

"Okay, so make yourself comfortable while I get the kids fed and I'll come back and show you around." The woman paused at the doorway. "I'm hoping you'll come work with me this morning. Meet the children."

12

Things were going too fast for Angel. Out of control. She'd been way more scared when she was literally running from Scotty but at least she was on her own. She was used to that. She wasn't used to having anyone actually take care of her. It had usually been the other way around. Reassuring her mother, giving her advice, helping her pick outfits, painting her nails and putting finishing touches on her makeup. The only thing her mom had been in charge of was the two or three hours of school reading every day. Her mom's dad had been a teacher before he left the family for another woman, and her mom had always regretted running away on her own before she finished high school.

Angel needed to plan. Get out alone where she understood

the rules. She couldn't stay with Rita for a number of reasons. First, she would be too visible in this tiny town. Second, Rita couldn't afford her own family, let alone another mouth to feed. Angel had walked into the kitchen and seen the kids' breakfast. White goo. "Mush," Rita had said. "Nutritious, want some?" Angel could tell that no one who wasn't broke would eat that stuff.

She didn't want to seem ungrateful after all the help that Ramón and Momo and Rita had given her. She wouldn't leave today. Tomorrow night. She'd write a thanks note. Today she'd walk the town, see if she could scrounge some things she needed. Better-fitting shoes. Water jug. Backpack. Maybe even matches. And a map. She had to at least look at a map. Find the closest city. Disappear. When she felt safe again she would think about calling the police.

SHE TRIED TO BEG OFF going with Rita to Head Start. Rita wouldn't hear of it. When she and Rita and the youngest, Jessie, went out the front door, Momo's pickup was gone. Vincente had the truck cab tipped up and was doing something to the engine. He leaned out when Jessie yelled good-bye.

"Momo says take care," he shouted to Angel. "Says he'll come visit on his way back to Ramón's in a few days." He blew Rita a kiss and turned back to the engine.

"Classroom's only a block or so down around the corner," Rita said, as Jessie took off running ahead of them. "I got fifteen kids from around here. Got an aide, LaDonna, who makes the snacks and plays nurse and helps with the teaching when she can. It'll be great to have another set of hands, and these kids can use extra attention."

Angel nodded to be polite but the thought of being around a bunch of children made her uncomfortable. What was she supposed to do? What would she say to a four-year-old?

As if reading her mind, Rita touched her lightly on the shoulder. "Don't worry. They're real sweet. Doing this kind of work made me keep wanting more kids. Till I got up to three and came to my senses." She looked at Angel and smiled. "Not that I think you'll want to have kids right away. Take a month or two before you start your own family!"

Angel knew she was being teased but didn't know how to respond. Her mom hadn't teased, and the men made everything sexual.

Rita went on to tell Angel the children's names and something brief about each one and then they were there, unlocking the door. The building might have originally been a small church or an old one-room school. Immediately inside was a square hall where Angel imagined the kids could put their jackets or lunch sacks. Leaving the anteroom, they walked into a large rectangular high-ceilinged area with a scratched wood floor and a fair amount of natural light from tall dirty windows. Four battered folding tables were evenly spaced on the right side of the room, leaving an open area on the left side large enough for exercise or games. More scarred tables holding plastic storage containers lined each side wall, and at the back Angel could see what she thought was a food-service counter closed by a rolling metal shutter.

"That's our kitchen," Rita said, pointing to the back. "La-Donna will be here in a few minutes, so let's set out some glasses and plates, napkin by each setting, four kids to a table."

ANGEL NODDED WHEN INTRODUCED TO THE CHILDREN, sat and watched the activities during the morning, didn't eat, didn't play. She couldn't keep her mind off Scotty. Where could she grab supplies and a map without alerting Rita to her flight plans? If she could walk to a different highway system, away from 10 and 86, that would be perfect. Scotty couldn't cover every place. Then she could hitchhike and maybe get out of state. Gone for good.

She was considering searching the glove compartment in Rita's Toyota, maybe even Vincente's truck for a road map, when a commotion interrupted her reverie. The largest girl in class was being pulled kicking and punching from a chubby light-skinned boy. Rita lifted the girl in a bear hug and was whispering to her as she carried her to the table nearest Angel.

"Looks like Norma may have had a difficult night and came to school pretty frustrated," Rita said, placing the girl in a chair and sitting next to her. "It's okay to feel angry but it's not all right to hurt anyone when you feel that way," Rita said, looking at Angel but clearly intending her remarks for Norma. "Have you felt angry lately?" Rita asked Angel.

Angel, surprised, nodded.

"How did you deal with it?"

Angel didn't like being put on the spot, didn't like being drawn into this situation, but thought about the question anyway. "I ran, I guess," she said.

"Did that work?" Rita asked her. "Did that help you deal with the anger or feel better?"

Angel hadn't thought about it. "Not really."

"Here at school we're learning to talk about how we're feeling and see if that—"

"I ain't talking to nobody," Norma interrupted.

Rita ignored her. "You have somebody really really mad at you, right?" she asked Angel.

Angel's mouth came open as she fought the impulse to tell Rita to get bent. She knew Rita was trying to work with the girl but this was way over the top. Looking for something to say, Angel noticed Norma's eyes on her. "Uh, yeah."

"How do you feel when someone is really mad at you?" Rita asked.

"Scared," Angel replied without thinking.

"You don't got to be escared," Norma said. "Scaredy Cat. You're big. Can't nobody hurt you."

"Anybody can hurt anybody if they want to bad enough," Angel said, a little heat in her own voice.

"Can even big people be scared?" Rita asked, still looking at Angel.

A buzzer went off, momentarily distracting the three of them.

"Lunch is ready," Rita explained. "You two sit here for five more minutes," she said, handing Norma her watch. "See this long hand? When it moves to here, you and Angel can come over. If you forget, Angel can help you."

Angel watched Rita move across the room and tell the others to clean up their games and go wash hands. She could feel Norma staring at her but she didn't look. She didn't know what she was supposed to do.

"You're too big for this school," Norma said. "Have you been bad too?"

Angel smiled in spite of herself. "Sometimes," she said, looking at her lap.

"What?" Norma asked, turning to face Angel directly.

Angel searched her memory for a decent example. "Ruined all my mom's lipsticks when she said I couldn't wear any. Stole money from her purse," Angel said, noticing a growing sadness as she thought about being her mother's child.

Norma drew in a dramatic breath like those examples were impossibly naughty. "My dad would kill me if I stole," she said, making her eyes comically wide.

"That's not funny," Angel said, regretting it. She didn't need to make this girl feel bad.

Norma looked away, then down, seemingly sorry she didn't please the older girl. She stayed quiet for a minute. "My dad hit my mom last night and made her mouth bleed," she said.

ANGEL TRIED TO BE FOCUSED DURING LUNCH, offering kids more milk when their cups were empty, replacing dropped napkins, getting another half sandwich for anyone who was still hungry. She wasn't going to eat, but her growling stomach was entertaining the kids at her table so she downed a sandwich. She reminded herself that she'd need food for when she took off. The kids talked and laughed with one another, didn't speak to her. Norma, she noticed, sat at the place Rita saved at a table with all girls.

After lunch, story time, after that, nap. Angel spaced on the story, looking back over her own childhood and the times she saw a man hit her mother. So many times. When the children were either sleeping or eyes closed, quiet, Rita motioned for Angel to join her in the kitchen.

"Thanks for helping me with Norma," she said, sitting on a high stool so she could see the children as they rested on the mats in the other room. "That girl's got a load to pull. Dad's in counseling for domestic violence with the wife and sexually abusing Norma's older sister. He may have already gotten to Norma. Mother was in the refuge down in Brawley for a month and came back to the guy when she got out. Norma sees what goes on. What can she make of this world? Everybody's a target for her rage, every child's afraid of her, and she is so desperate to be liked . . . to be loved. It breaks my heart."

Too much. Too many feelings. Angel stood and left without speaking.

BEFORE SHE WALKED BACK TO RITA'S to search for a map, Angel wandered nearby looking for places she could take cover on a moment's notice. The good thing about Salt Shores? There were thousands of places to hide: sheds, empty trailers, crumbling boats. In the middle of a vacant lot next to the school sat a rusted yellow bus with broken windows, and perpendicular to it an old delivery truck somebody had lived in. Close beside, a couple of dead cars with rotting upholstery and flat tires. Any of them could provide quick shelter.

As she sized them up, she did not imagine that four other vehicles were similarly parked fifty miles north in a paved lot near a Cathedral City gun shop. A locksmith's panel truck, a ratty Chevy Suburban, and a silver Cadillac rested while the drivers stood around a camo-colored pickup and hatched a plan with their occasional business partner.

THAT EVENING ANGEL HELPED RITA wash the dinner dishes. Least she could do for the meal. "Norma cried most of the afternoon. Thought she drove you away," Rita said, standing beside Angel, drying plates. "I'm not telling you to make you feel bad. I'm just saying what a strong effect we have on these kids."

Angel continued her silence. Didn't break it till after dark when she asked Rita if it was safe to go for a walk around the streets.

"Vincente don't like it when I do that but he's driving for the next four days. Go ahead. People don't close their doors or windows. Yell if you need something. You stay in the open, you should be fine. I have to walk sometimes, too."

By day, ghost town, by night, village. Angel took the right that led past Head Start and continued east toward the sea. Some ramshackle houses were completely dark, probably empty, but many others showed dim lights, flickering TVs, once in a while yelling or laughter. Angel noticed the deserted places, made a mental note to come back tomorrow and check them for usable supplies.

As she neared the Marina Club parking lot she could hear a jukebox mixed up with noise from a TV program and snatches of talk, occasional hoots like somebody scored or won a bet. On the beach at the end of the lot she was puzzled by a line of cars and SUVs parked beside walls that looked like reed huts. Closer, she could tell these were partially enclosed campsites occupied by couples or families out on a cheap holiday.

Could you swim in this sea? Was it polluted? Were there fish? There were birds. A silent glide of pelicans drifted by, wings intermittently reflecting shore lights. A heron looking like an unemployed butler stood patiently at the end of a sandbar. Must be something edible in there.

She continued south along the water's edge past empty-looking fabricated buildings, storage or perhaps an abandoned plant of some kind. Taking the next street west toward the highway, she reentered the residential section and methodically worked her way back and forth till she believed she'd seen the whole town.

Rita was in the living room reading when Angel returned. "Work it out?" she asked.

Angel shrugged.

"Find what you were looking for?"

Did Rita suspect? Probably. She seemed like a hard woman to fool.

"Would you do something for me?" Rita asked. "You got no reason to. You don't owe me anything. I'm just asking."

Angel dreaded moments like this. Way easier to be alone than to have somebody want something of you. Her mom had bled her dry. All she could do now, if she could even do that much, was save herself. She didn't have a thing to give to anyone else. Not even if they deserved it. Norma flashed to mind and she fought away the image.

"Give me the rest of the week," Rita asked. "Work and the kids . . . keep me company, help me out till Vincente gets back. I know you got big trouble chasing you, but I think you're safe here. What do you—"

Crying from another room interrupted her and she rose to see who'd had a nightmare or fallen out of bed. If Angel had had a chance to talk, she would have refused, but the interruption seemed like fate. Okay, just a few days. And by doing that she felt like she could ask Rita to help her find traveling supplies.

13

The next day by morning snack time, Angel was helping with the children. After snack she joined the show-and-tell and at her turn produced the piece of emery board she still carried. "When you get older you use one of these to keep your fingernails smooth," she told fourteen unimpressed children and a rapt Norma, who hadn't taken her eyes off Angel since she'd arrived.

When it was time for games, the only one Angel remembered was checkers. She set up the board and sat waiting for a partner. No one came. Norma was in a corner playing alone with blocks. After a few minutes Angel noticed a blond boy edging closer to her but every time she looked at him he stopped moving and looked away. Angel glanced at Norma. Norma was homed in on the boy's advance and getting to her feet. Uh-oh.

And then Rita was in the block corner towing Norma to Angel's table.

"I wonder if you could teach this big girl how to play checkers?" she asked Norma.

"Everybody knows how to play checkers," Norma said, looking away toward the windows.

"Maybe," Rita said, "but maybe not everybody remembers."

Norma darted a look at Angel. "You?" she asked. "You 'member?"

"She hasn't played in a long time," Rita said. "Would you help?"

Norma sat.

At lunch Norma joined Angel's group. And offered her an apple slice. And at story time she sat almost near enough to touch.

During nap time Angel and Rita again sat together in the kitchen. "She looks relieved," Rita said, munching on a celery stick.

"She told me she and her mom and sister are going to win a million dollars," Angel said. "Told me her mom bought a lucky ticket yesterday at the StopShop."

"Did you ask her what she would do if she won?"

"No, but she told me. Go to Disneyland. Live there."

"Oh, me. She's why we need an after-school program when kids start kindergarten."

"How about a pistol? Shoot the dads. Be cheaper." Angel was surprised by her rage. Better keep a lid on it. People might think she was crazy.

Rita adjusted her butt on the stool so she could see the children better. "If all of us shoot the people we don't like, will there be anybody left?"

Angel stifled a bitter reply. Asked instead, "Would it really matter?"

Rita went on, "Sometimes when I'm pretty low I don't think it matters. Misery don't care. But when I'm feeling loved, or when I look at my kids and these children, it matters."

Feeling loved? Angel knew she was her mother's only friend. Thirty times a day her mom needed her for something. But it sure didn't feel like love. Real love was a fairy tale.

Angel looked across the room where Norma was sleeping, curled, arm over face, still as the moon. She hoped Norma would have a decent life, would have a better life than she had today, but that didn't mean she loved her. No, Angel didn't love anybody. Didn't know how. From nowhere Abuela came to mind. Abuela thought up the escape; the change-clothes thing at the church that knocked Scotty off the trail. Kind of amazing, really. Old, smart, tough in her own way. And Ramón, strong and kind. Rita, the same. If she ever had the chance, could she love people like that? Could they ever . . . she made herself stop.

DINNER THAT NIGHT WAS A COUPLE OF DRY TORTILLAS and a couple of tablespoons of refried beans for each person. Nobody complained, but Rita's youngest boy kept staring at Angel's plate as if wishing he could add it to his own. No comparison to the feast at Ramón's. Angel decided that tonight on her walk she'd also look for cans and bottles she could trade in for a candy bar she could give to the kids. After she finished drying the dishes she left while Rita put the kids to bed.

The streets were quiet except for radio music coming from the garages where men worked or drank beer with their friends. A faded brown house looked gray in the sliver of moonlight, and Angel walked the overgrown path to the front door, which stood open a couple of inches. Inside, two dining room chairs faced each other, table missing. Plastic garbage and food wrappers covered the floor. Looked like homeless occasionally used this place. Probably nothing left of value.

Out the side door a carport was walled by torn bamboo shades and tarps. Inside were empty oil containers, greasy rags, and a rusted push mower. In back, under what was probably once the workbench, she found a screwdriver. Weapon. You never know. Just having it in her jeans pocket made her feel safer. Scattered here and there were some unbroken glass bottles and aluminum cans. She gathered them in a discarded plastic shopping bag and continued her search down the block. If she could fill that bag and one more she might be able to cash them in for a Hershey.

WHITE MOTHS SKITTERED AROUND the StopShop's neon sign. Parked near the front door where light was brightest, a pale blue clunker served as a bench for five or six teens in shorts and tanks, no one Angel had seen before. The two girls leaned

69

against their guys, drinking beer and giggling. What would that be like?

Angel was careful to stay out of their sight line. She brushed at the flies cruising around the Dumpster and braced herself against the sour smell. The lid creaked when she opened it but not loud enough to attract attention. Near the top of the pile beneath some paper soda cups and crushed milk cartons she found two old sandwiches still in their wrappers. Opened one. It didn't stink and the mayo and mustard were in foil packets. Could be okay. She stuck the food inside her shirt to try later. Deeper, she spotted a treasure. A small nylon gym bag with wrinkled shorts and stiff socks that must have fallen out of some car and gotten tossed. She shook the underwear into the receptacle and inspected her find. Not bad. Now she could carry a little water and a change of clothes when she took off.

She could see a case of empty brown beer bottles on the bottom but she couldn't reach it and she didn't want to climb in and totally stink up her clothes. While she searched she was dimly aware of the occasional buzz of cars passing on the highway a hundred feet west beyond the parking lot. The all-night safety light on a tall pole at the edge of the blacktop hummed, and the Dumpster creaked with her weight as she shifted position, but over those sounds she picked up the low rumble of an exhaust pipe. She knew that sound. Ducking behind the receptacle, she watched a heavy camo pickup roll into the lot and park next to the clunker. She leaned over and coughed a thin gruel of refried beans onto the blacktop.

14

Angel burst in the front door breathless from running. First thing she noticed was the silence: no soft radio, no snores from the kids' rooms, no noise from the kitchen, where Rita would be preparing food or putting together things for school tomorrow. *Did he come here first?*

Angel made herself open the door to the room Jessie shared with her sister. The beds were empty. Tried the boy's room. The same. Angel raced to Rita's bedroom and found her throwing clothes in a daypack. Frantic. Angel cleared her throat and Rita jumped.

"Ramón called," Rita said, glancing at her and then turning back to her packing. "Matteo's missing."

"Matteo?" Angel thought about the Gomez boy in the UCLA T-shirt who had been so obviously irritated at her intrusion a couple of days ago. Wanted to give her up to Scotty.

"He didn't come back last night. Hasn't phoned and no one's seen him. Tío spoke to Ramón, said the boy may have gone over to their home to get some things for school. Your guy may have caught him there."

A wave of guilt washed Angel against the door frame. She should have warned them better. Poison. Everyone who came near her was going to get hurt. She gathered herself and approached Rita.

"Stop." She put her hand on Rita's arm to still the packing. "You can't go. You got your kids."

"They're with friends. He can't find them." She cast around the room, spotted a flashlight standing on her night table and tossed that in. "Ramón said the guy could know about me now," Rita said, rushing, distracted. "None of the Gomez family ever visited, so Matteo couldn't tell him much more than my name and the town, but that guy'll find out where I live as soon as he asks. Everybody knows me."

"He's already here," Angel said, hating to bring worse news. "At the StopShop." Angel grimaced, remembering Scotty's oily charm. "Won't take him long."

"Get the lights." Rita raked the room with her eyes one more time before she shouldered the daypack. "You go out the back. Go through the yards to the school. I'll pick you up in a couple of minutes."

Angel wanted to argue but there was no time. She'd learned that. Scotty was too quick. Moving through the kitchen, Angel took a second to open the fridge. Water. She wouldn't forget again. But Rita didn't buy water. Angel gave up and bolted outside.

She climbed through a broken fence into the neighbor's place and, despite dogs barking in a couple of houses, made her way to the side street. Seeing no people, nothing moving, she stayed low and used parked cars and tall weeds to cover her two-block run to the school. In less than a minute Rita's Toyota barreled down the street and slowed enough for Angel to jump in.

"I got an idea," Rita said, making a hard left at the next block and then another, heading back toward the street she lived on.

"Don't!" Angel yelled, fighting a swirling panic. "He'll see us. He'll hurt you."

"Hang on," Rita said, concentrating on driving with her lights off. "I know a place to watch from."

Angel was sorry she had gotten in the car. Rita would be better off without her. Angel reached for the door handle.

"Don't even think it," Rita said, slowing and turning into a driveway. She pulled into an empty garage, jumped out, and ran around to move a rickety gate closed enough to hide the vehicle. Angel was still in the front seat, locked with indecision, when Rita opened the car door and took her hand. "If we don't see headlights, we're crossing the street."

Angel tried to tug away but Rita's grip was strong. "No way," Rita said. "Help me spot him."

They ran to the corner and crouched behind thistles looking

toward Rita's house a block to their left on the cross street. No headlights, nothing moving. Rita put her arm around Angel, stood, and started across the intersection. "Act natural," she said. "We're going to that empty white place."

Angel could hardly stand it. This was so stupid. They had to run. Run! But she walked with Rita, her body agreeing to what her mind refused. When they reached the weeds by the front porch, Angel's knees gave way, as if going against her strongest instincts had paralyzed her.

"We can get on the walkway from the backyard," Rita said, hauling Angel to her feet and sneaking along the side of the building.

Rita's words made no sense. Angel needed to gather her strength to break free.

Behind the house were more weeds and the tumbled remains of a brick barbecue. But along the far edge of the yard sat a tall rusted metal staircase that wound in a spiral toward the top of the house. "I think this is the tallest platform in town," Rita said, as she led Angel to the very steep steps that disappeared in the dark above the roofline. "Don't stand when we get up there. Crawl to the front edge," Rita said. "We can see everything from there."

Angel's resistance faded. Things were so messed up it was hard to keep trying. Matteo. Soon maybe Rita, too. Angel wasn't worth it. Wasn't worth the trouble she was causing. It felt like something inside was crumbling, washing away. When Rita told her to climb, she did without argument. A fall was as good a way to die as any.

The railing was gritty, hard to hold. Even in the darkness Angel could see her hands were getting filthy. When she looked down, Rita was inching up right below, close enough to catch her if she slipped. *Why is she risking all this for me? Because I've trapped her.*

Angel stopped climbing, looked down over her shoulder. "You don't have to do this. Get out of here. Save your family."

Rita didn't look up. "Climb now, talk later," she said, poking Angel in the butt. "Move, girl."

Slowly, taking more care, Angel made it to a metal grate that formed an edge around the roof.

"Get on up," Rita said. "Watch out for the furniture so you don't knock anything over, and slide yourself across to the edge by the street. It's like a deck."

Angel had never seen anything like this before, a platform where a roof ought to be, but it was mostly flat except for some buckling where the plywood seams came together. Looking ahead she saw a thin-legged table surrounded by a few folding chairs. More chairs were strewn around the deck as if a storm had knocked them over. A tiny barbecue not much bigger than a cinder block sat near the table close to a couple of milk crates. She looked to be above everything but the palm trees. Okay, she got it. If she stood she would be a silhouette that could be seen by anyone.

When she reached the front edge, the town spread below her. Lights peeking out windows in the occupied houses seemed like holiday decorations. She could see all the way to the shore and the dark water beyond. A short distance to her right, past Rita's house, three street lamps marked the main road in from the highway and the StopShop glowed with a soft neon rainbow that was almost festive. The store's parking area was halfway screened by the building, but she didn't see anything that looked like Scotty's pickup.

She looked in the yards below for anyone with a flashlight or anyone smoking a cigarette but the homes and streets seemed deserted as usual. *Maybe he left.* She felt Rita move close, turned to watch her prop on her elbows, heard her groan with the effort.

"Now we watch," Rita said, still getting her breathing quieted.

"I'm sorry," Angel said, but maybe it was too soft for Rita to hear. Angel bit her lip until she tasted blood. She kept getting caught off guard. How dumb was she? She hadn't done one thing right. Should have kept running. Now it was too complicated because Rita couldn't run. Her whole family was going to pay big-time.

"Did you bring a phone?" Angel asked.

Rita reached for her handbag but stopped. "In the car," she said. She shook her head. "Too scared to think right."

Angel thought she could see water in the corners of Rita's eyes. *She's so beautiful.* She reached for Rita's hand but froze as headlights turned off the main road onto their street.

A pickup moved slowly toward them, too slowly, and stopped in front of Rita's house. The headlights went out, the driver's door popped open, and a man ran at full speed through Rita's driveway and into her backyard. The sound of wood splintering carried softly up to where they lay. The house lights came on. While they were straining to hear more, Rita's front door burst open and the man strode out to his truck, looking north and south along the road. When he stopped moving and became very still, Angel knew. Scotty. First scan for movement, then get quiet and listen. Just like he'd described, telling her how to hunt. Travel till you run across their track, make tighter circles till you find them.

SCOTTY STAYED IN THE STREET FOR SEVERAL MINUTES, moving only to reach in and turn off the truck. First he faced north, looking toward the edge of town and the house where they perched. Angel could feel Rita tense and wondered whether they were back-lit and visible. He didn't look up.

After a minute he turned to look east. Angel resumed breathing. The town spread in that direction five or six blocks to the sea. Head Start was one block past his truck and two down, but he may not have known that, may not have asked about it. On the other side of the pickup, to the west, the land was mostly open desert with very few buildings. Angel watched as he took off his cap and rubbed his hair with his arm. The night wasn't that hot. He'd probably worked up a sweat breaking into Rita's.

Finally, he climbed in the pickup, started it, and rolled backwards to a dirt rut near where Vincente's semi had been parked, about a quarter-mile across bare ground from the highway and the StopShop parking lot. *He's leaving!* But he wasn't. He turned and continued backing two or three hundred feet onto the path, braked, and shut off the engine. He could sit in the truck and watch Rita's home. The house platform was now peripheral, off to his left. Angel was pretty sure he couldn't see them.

"Do you think he has night goggles?" Rita asked.

Angel's relief evaporated.

"We better cross again. Get the phone," Rita said. "He can't see us in the street from his angle." Rita pushed herself on her stomach back to the edge with the stairs. Angel watched as she swung her legs off the roof and moved carefully to place her feet back on the steps.

Angel hesitated, aware of a strong urge to just lie still; hide, sleep. Let Rita save herself. Again Rita must have read her mind. She returned, took hold of Angel's sleeve, and towed her the first couple of feet, sliding back to the stairs.

THE GARAGE WHERE THEY'D HIDDEN THE CAR smelled sharp, rank. Cat spray, rat pee, who knew what else. Angel levered herself in through the open passenger window. No sense opening the door and triggering the light if she didn't have to. Rita dug her purse out of the seat and found the cell phone. Walked to the edge of the garage door to keep watch on the street.

"TJ? Rita. Hey, I got trouble. Serious. Guy's after a friend of mine. Broke in my house."

It was so dark inside the garage that Angel could see the glow of the cell phone, and she listened while a male voice buzzed through the receiver. When she couldn't follow the man's side of the conversation, she sank back in the seat, unable to concentrate, unable to keep her eyes open. She jerked when Rita started the car.

"Let's wait at LaDonna's," Rita said, twisting to look out the rear window.

Bad idea. Angel knew it. They'd be visible again, moving, maybe brake lights. "He could see us," she told Rita. "If Scotty asked what you drive, if he knows your car, he could find us when you stop."

Rita didn't answer. She hunched over the steering wheel, careful, quiet, slow-rolling out of the driveway, shifting, gliding away at idle speed.

LaDonna answered the door in a soft pink nightgown, hair in curlers, pillow creases on her face. She let them in and nodded toward the couch. "What's going on? You okay?" she asked. "Fight with Vince?"

"Weird school parent," Rita said. "No big deal. We just don't want to be hassled anymore tonight."

"You safe?" LaDonna asked. "Want me to wake Ricky?"

"No. Let him sleep. We're fine. We'll rest here a bit and then we'll lock up when we leave. And, hey, there's some chance you'll need to open school tomorrow."

"Whatever," LaDonna said, turning. "You want anything, kitchen's yours." She nodded toward the room on her left as she padded away. "You need anything, call me."

"Gutierrez checked him out, let him go before I got your call. Far as we can tell, he's left town."

Angel opened her eyes to see a man in a khaki uniform and cowboy boots, flat-brimmed hat in hand, speaking to Rita, who was seated on the couch beside her.

"Guy said he got sleepy driving. Pulled off the highway, found that open area to take a nap," the man said, rolling and unrolling his hat brim. "Gutierrez checked his plates, license. No warrants. Guy pulled out and drove off." The man shook his head. "Goot's been off a few days. Wife's sick."

Rita nodded her head. "Inez? I heard. Chemo?"

The officer nodded. "Looks bad. Anyway, Goot missed the heads-up from Cathedral City. This guy fits the person of interest in a federal investigation over by Joshua Tree."

"He killed my mother." Angel couldn't believe she said it. Sleepy, groggy, stupid. She could feel Rita looking at her while she herself studied the brown man's face. He was hard to read but Angel didn't think he believed her. Or maybe he just didn't hear what she said. The extended silence told her she was wrong. He heard her. He thought she was a liar and wasn't sure how to respond.

"Your name?" he asked. "You made a report? Filed charges?"

Angel said nothing.

He shifted his gaze to Rita for a cue.

"This guy's been chasing her. Tore up my house looking for her," Rita said. "Something pretty serious happened."

"Yeah, well, that's a serious charge," he said, looking back at Angel. "Evidence?" he asked her.

She thought about it. Trailer burned. If he moved her mom's grave . . . She shook her head.

"Maybe you ought to think it over before you say things like that to a law officer. False charges get you in trouble." He looked at her for a moment longer. "You already in trouble?"

"She's been helping me at the preschool," Rita said. "Take a look at my house. We haven't been back but we saw the guy go in. Heard him break things. The guy's stalking her. She's underage. You got to stop that."

Angel pushed herself to a sitting position so she wouldn't seem like a child.

"You sure it's the same guy? You weren't home at the time, right? You can make a positive I.D.? What color's his hair?"

Rita looked away.

"That's what I thought," he said.

"Brown, green eyes," Angel said.

"That's pretty good night vision at a distance," the man said, looking up and away as if he found LaDonna's curtain rod interesting.

"Hey, TJ, cut her some slack," Rita said, putting her arm around Angel's shoulders. "She's been through a lot."

They were distracted by LaDonna entering the room, now wearing a quilted robe and a scarf over her curlers.

"What's going on?" she asked Rita, as she came to stand by the couch.

"Not much, honey," Rita said, putting her other hand over LaDonna's on the sofa arm. "TJ's just helping us deal with a nutcase that's been following Angel. We're trying to get it squared away," she said, standing to join LaDonna.

"So, it wasn't a parent?"

Rita shook her head.

"He's coming here?" LaDonna looked back toward her bedroom, alarmed.

"He's gone," TJ said.

"He doesn't know we came here," Rita said. "He left town. It's okay."

Angel made herself be still, face blank. Scotty might have driven off, but it wasn't okay. Not even close. And it was getting worse.

ANGEL FOLLOWED RITA AND TJ OUT TO THE STREET.

"Just to make sure you two are safe," TJ said, opening the squad car door, "and I want to see the house damage. Maybe we need to put a BOLO on this guy." He noticed the look of confusion on Rita's face. "Be on the lookout," he explained.

She nodded.

"We'll give this guy another scan. Call Cathedral and see if they're still interested." He offered Rita his hand and helped her follow Angel into the backseat.

"He catches eagles and sells them," Angel said, but the noise of the car door shutting covered her words. She had very bad feelings about getting into the back of a sheriff's car, even for a two-block ride. She was starting to get caught in the system and the system was going to get her killed.

15

I know you're tired, but we need to talk." Rita was standing directly in front of Angel in the middle of her living room, where they'd waited while TJ investigated the break-in damage.

Angel could see TJ's cruiser through the living room blinds. He'd left telling them not to touch the doorknobs or light switches. Said he'd have a lab person come tomorrow morning and check for prints. Said he'd wait outside till a female deputy arrived to spend the night.

"Talk tomorrow," Angel said. "I'm wiped."

"No. No way," Rita, adamant. "You'll wait till I sleep and then you'll run? I don't want to stay up all night neither, but I have to know what all's happened, what you think this guy'll do next. I need my own plan. Protect my kids. And hear this clear," she said. "I really like you and I don't want you to leave. I—do—not—want—you—to—leave."

Angel looked away from her to the front door, picturing walking out and wondering what TJ would do if she did. "You've seen it," she told Rita, trying to decide if the front door was dead-bolted. "He's chasing me. When I disappear for good, he's home free. Mom had no family, I got no family. Nobody wanted either of us. We were there for the taking. Scotty knew that."

Angel was antsy to get on her way but she didn't want to seem obvious. She took her eyes off the door and surveyed the nearby furniture like she wanted to sit.

Rita walked over and steered Angel to the love seat by the standing lamp, where she often read stories aloud to her children. She sat as Angel sat and angled herself till they were touching knees. "So tell me," she said.

Okay, no rush, Angel thought. *In a while I'll say I have to pee and I'll go out the bathroom window.* She closed her eyes and was quiet for a minute, uncomfortable about retrieving those memories. "When this all started I wasn't ready. For any of it. I just knew I didn't want to die. I wanted to kill him for what he did." Angel felt in her jeans pockets, made sure the folded money was still there. She looked back to Rita. "I don't care so much now, either way, but I don't want to take anybody with me. No need for anybody else to . . ." She stopped, not knowing how to end the sentence.

Rita waited.

"We'd only been with him a few weeks and every night he

and Mom would drink and snort stuff and fight. If he was loaded and Mom locked him out of the bedroom, he would come to get with me. I started leaving the trailer and sleeping outside." She rested her head against the back of the couch and let the story spool into the room, floodwater slowly pushing over a door's threshold.

After Angel told the part about Scotty burning the trailer and nearly killing her, Rita leaned over and smoothed Angel's forehead with her thumbs. Ran her fingers lightly over the healing burns and scrapes on Angel's face. "Why don't we take a little break?" Rita said, her voice as soft and smooth as her fingers. "Let's go to the bathroom, get some juice . . . "

They did, both in the small room together, one finger-combing her hair in the mirror while the other finished. Angel knew this messed up her plan to leave but she was tired and she knew another opportunity would come up, maybe when the woman deputy arrived.

Rita listened to the rest of the story, not interrupting with questions, and making a sound only once: a chuckle when Angel told how Abuela fooled Scotty by swapping clothes at the church. When Angel was done, Rita rolled her head around her shoulders, loosening her neck, and took a long breath.

"That's a lot more trouble than I imagined," Rita said, "more than anyone should have to go through."

"There's probably a lot worse happens everywhere," Angel said. "I'm still breathing and he didn't get on me that last time."

"You know if you leave, he'll find you," Rita said. "That's what he does."

"Yeah, well, I run. That's what I do. Easier to hide than find."

"Not much of a life," Rita said.

Angel shrugged.

"And there's another thing you're kind of losing track of," Rita said.

It didn't matter to Angel but she said "What" because the rhythm of the conversation was soothing.

"You can't do it alone. Alone you'll die, 'cause you don't have any resource. If you steal, sooner or later you'll get caught and he'll get you."

All these words. Angel was having trouble making herself pay attention.

"So you have to bring other people into it," Rita said. "How many so far?"

Angel heard that all right. Not good. Didn't want to think about it. She started to get up and was stopped by Rita's hand.

"You're tough. We both know it," Rita said, "but how many people you brought into this?"

Angel tore her arm out of Rita's grasp.

"What's it cost so far?" Rita asked, shifting until she could look right into Angel's face.

"That's not my fault. I didn't ask for help." Angel could hear how loud she was getting and jammed her fingernails into her palms for the control that pain would bring.

"What about Matteo? What about Celina's car and the

Gomez livestock?" Rita asked, her voice gentle against Angel's volume. "Gomez family chose to pay that price?"

Angel stood and Rita stood with her.

"Ramón, Carmen, Momo, me, Vincente, Jessie? We just fence posts you running past? Too bad if we got trouble? You just doing what you got to? We pay our money, take our risk, tough titty if we don't like it?"

"Shut up!" Angel didn't want to hit her but she might.

"You a little like Scotty? No heart, no conscience? Owe nobody nothing? Everyone for himself?"

That was way too much. She was not like Scotty. Never like Scotty. Never in a million years.

"Are you nuts?" Angel's voice echoed. She glanced out the window to see if TJ was getting out of his car. "You know I'm not—" Surprise tears washed from her eyes, ran from her nose, collapsed her words into staccato hiccups. She wanted to stay on her feet but her wail took all her energy and she fell against Rita, pounding at her chest. Rita stepped inside the blows and Angel's punches went wide, glancing off Rita's shoulders. Rita held the girl tightly, turning her face to the side so Angel wouldn't butt her.

WHEN THE DEPUTY ARRIVED WITHIN THE HOUR, she found them on the floor, Rita wrapped around Angel, arms and legs, like you'd hold an enraged four-year-old to keep her from hurting herself during a tantrum. The woman walked them to Rita's bedroom, covered them with a blanket, put a chair outside their door, and sat waiting for daybreak.

* * *

NOT LONG AFTER DAWN, Rita woke and brewed coffee for the deputy. Took a shower and made phone calls. Checked in from time to time to see that Angel was still sleeping. When she finished these chores, she made the deputy a fried-egg sandwich. She herself would eat later with Angel.

"Would you ask TJ to give us one more day of protection?" she asked the deputy when she collected her plate. The woman nodded and got on her cell phone.

ANGEL ROSE AND CLEANED UP while a lab tech dusted the doors and light switches. When she was ready she joined Rita at the kitchen table and wolfed down her sandwich. She noticed Rita looking her over, appraising. Angel had chosen clothes from Rita's closet that would be good for travel: two T-shirts under a brown hoodie, cargo pants, battered running shoes. Different from the thin polo shirt and long shorts she'd worn the previous day.

"Find everything you needed?" Rita asked, voice level.

Angel blushed, nodded.

"I called LaDonna, and she's doing school today," Rita went on. "Another mom's coming in and they'll go to the beach, get wet, pick up things for collages. We'll stay here. I want you to tell me more about Scotty."

"I don't want to think about him," Angel said, twisting her hair.

"You remember what you told me? You're good at running and hiding? To be good at hiding you have to know who's

looking for you, what they'll think, what they'll do." Rita put
their plates in the sink and refilled her coffee. "It's kind of automatic, most times you don't even notice you're doing it."

"I guess." Angel yawned, retied her shoe, giving off signs
that she really wasn't into this. When she'd acted this way with
her mom, her mom would get mad and pout and leave her
alone. Angel needed space to make her break.

"So what's Scotty like?" Rita persisted, sitting again, facing
Angel directly.

Angel sighed. "Well, I told Tío and Abuela, he's a hunter.
And I told what's-his-name that Scotty traps tortoise and eagles and sells them."

"On the black market?"

"I don't know where," Angel said, irritated, letting Rita
know these questions were annoying. "To hunt those things
you got to be patient, really organized. Which is kind of
odd 'cause Scotty's not patient except in that one area. He's
restless, sometimes kind of hyper. He doesn't like to wait for
things. Eats corn chips instead of making dinner. Same clothes
all the time unless he's going to town and slicks up kind of
country-western. He's real careful with the guns and traps,
but the rest of his stuff, like the trailer, too much trouble. I'm
the one who couldn't stand the mess, swept up, sacked up
garbage."

Angel rested her elbows on the table, not seeming to realize
that she was warming to the task. "At Mom's grave, I hid from
him, I knew I didn't have to go far 'cause he wouldn't spend
much time looking. He thought catching me'd be easy. I guess

it was, when he came back to the trailer." Angel winced at the memory.

"Now he knows I'm not alone. Knows I might get him locked up. He'll be way more sneaky. When he found me before at the Gomez place, real quick he knew I was there but he didn't do jack 'cause the scene was witnesses. He'd have to do everybody. But he didn't know them . . . like did they have family that'd come after him? Me and Mom were easy marks. Nobody knew us or knew where we were." Angel looked at her hands and saw she had torn her napkin into tiny pieces while she was talking.

"He broke in your house 'cause he thought he'd surprise us, deck you, grab me, get away. It'd happen so fast you couldn't even I.D. him. Bang, he'd be home free. Now that a police guy has seen him—"

"Sheriff's Department," Rita clarified. "TJ and Goot and the woman deputy staying here."

"Okay, a sheriff guy has seen him, so Scotty's got to be even slyer because his name and license are in the system. Now if anything happens to me or you, he's the main suspect, and Scotty wouldn't want that. He likes to be camo. You saw his truck. Under the . . . what is it?"

"Radar?" Rita supplied, nodding. Made sense.

"I don't think he'll hurt you or your kids, because it wouldn't be worth it. It would just up the stakes, get more people involved, and that could mess up his whole business."

Rita stood, went to the sink for a glass of water. Offered Angel one.

Angel shook her head. "Did I tell you he sells guns, too? If he hurt you, he'd have to disappear. Move. He probably doesn't think I'd rat him out, 'cause I'd wind up back in a foster house and he knows I hated that. I'm pretty sure he'll lay low for a while, let things die down, watch till he can get me alone. Bury me like he did Mom. That's why I have to get out of here. Get a head start . . . Hey, I get it." She smiled at Rita. "Your program. A head start. For regular school?"

Rita smiled back. "So Scotty buys and sells guns. All illegal."

"Says he usually steals them or gets them from a pawnshop guy, like a partner of his."

"Okay, he sells . . . more than just guns?"

"Other . . ."

"Weapons," Rita filled in.

"Yeah, uh, some tubes, rocket things, and some packages he says explode big-time."

"Steals things, sells weapons, and traps animals. Anything else?"

"Uh, uses dope. Pot, crystal. X. Stuff like that."

"Where does he get it?"

"I don't know."

"None of Scotty's business is legit?"

"A couple of times I've seen him fix a dead animal, like make it into a statue, and sell it. I don't know if that's legal."

"Taxidermy. Was he trained to do that? Did he go to school to learn that?"

"I don't know."

"Any other odd jobs?"

"He can fix a lot of things, his truck and stuff, but I don't think he does it for money."

"Does he have a regular house or a shop somewhere?" Rita asked, lifting a phone directory off the counter.

"Trailer's all I ever saw. He knows this area and has a bunch of guys he sells to."

"Never talked about parents or family. Brothers or sisters?"

"Uh-uh."

"So you don't think he'll try to hurt me or my kids?"

"No, I told you. Doesn't need to. He'll watch till he can grab—" Angel stopped abruptly, derailed. "Uh, I guess he might do you like the Gomez place. Wreck something. Your car, Vincente's truck. Or . . ." Angel mashed her hands to her forehead. "Or if I split, he might hurt you to get you to say where I went."

"So the best way for me and the kids to be safe is for you to stay here?"

Angel brought her fists down on the table with a bang that startled both of them. She stood suddenly, knocking her chair over, and ran out the back door with a wail that chain-sawed the quiet morning.

THE THIN MAN DRIVING the dirty gray Suburban had finished a quart of gin the night before, slept through his alarm, and arrived too late to see Angel leave the house alone. He spent a miserable morning parked in the Salt Shores sun and by afternoon was heading back to Cathedral City for medicinal beer.

ANGEL WOULDN'T BE ABLE TO CLEARLY RECALL where she went that day. Her memory would be mixed up and hazy like a home movie the trucker had sometimes shown her and her mother when they lived with him in Redding. The film had been cut and spliced and it jumped from scene to scene, place to place, changing characters and action so randomly it made no sense.

She knew at some point she had jogged along the uneven shoreline, scattering birds and making gouges in the wet sand. She recalled stumbling over grit and rock, plowing through shallow ravines, until she was near enough some paved road that she became afraid Scotty or a sheriff might see her. At one point she tripped and hit the ground hard enough to knock her wind out; she remembered lying there several minutes, coughing, furious and frustrated.

By nighttime she was sore and thirsty. She must have fallen more than that once, because her wrists ached and her palms were scratched and dotted with dark stickers. Why had she stopped moving? It took a moment to register that she stood facing the highway not far ahead. Vehicles shushing past on the asphalt, the white flash of headlights and the soft red trace of taillights offering a quiet light show in the dark blanket of desert.

Though she was not carrying it, she had found a map in

Rita's car a couple of days before when she'd walked out of the school in the early afternoon. She knew there was a bigger town about twenty miles to the south. She could have followed the seashore and been almost there by now. Maybe taken a bus to El Centro for three or four dollars. Maybe found a ride farther west, toward Escondido or San Diego. Disappeared. That's what she wanted, wasn't it? That's what she'd decided on, what she'd been working toward.

She thought back to her talk with Ramón. How would she get a job? Who would hire her? She'd have to lie about her age. Where could she live? How could she afford anything? But even as she recalled these questions she knew there was something else. Rita. Rita and her kids. Rita, who would be in danger because Scotty would think she knew where Angel went.

The night before, Rita had packed and run with her. Wouldn't let her go alone. Put herself on the line for Angel. Water slipped down Angel's cheeks. How many times had her mom sold her out? Taken a man's side against her? Every time but once, maybe? The day before her mother died, Angel had told her, "When you get mad and stomp out, Scotty comes to me." Is that what made the last fight so much worse? Did her mom unload on Scotty and keep at it so hard that he killed her to shut her up? Did her mom die trying to defend her? If Angel hadn't told, would her mom be alive now?

How much could a person hate herself? Was there a limit or at some point did a person explode like one of Scotty's bombs?

16

Angel passed a uniformed man seated behind the wheel of the cruiser parked in Rita's driveway. Goot? He didn't wave and she pretended to ignore him. The front door was unlocked. Rita sat on the love seat with Jessie and her boy, reading a story. They looked up but Angel didn't meet their eyes. She walked past them to the bathroom, washed the sand off her face and arms, searched for tweezers. She found them in the medicine cabinet and returned to the living room, to the chair nearest their reading lamp so she could see the thorns better.

When Rita put the children to bed, Angel was surprised by a gnawing hunger that surfaced without warning. The fridge had milk, eggs, Crisco, plastic containers of leftover rice and beans, a jar of red pepper salsa, and a vegetable bin that held cilantro and celery and old lettuce with brown edges. The cupboards had mostly glasses and dishes with only a small corner of enchilada sauces, boxes of cornmeal and pancake mix, a large paper sack of rice, a jar of peanut butter, and a ziplock bag of the white stuff that Angel had seen Rita use to make mush.

Angel decided on food her mother used to make, celery and peanut butter. She had just finished the snack when Rita walked in and took a chair at the table. Angel put the ingredients away and sat across from her. Rita handed her a thin napkin and gestured to her nose. Angel wiped off the dab of peanut butter. She crumpled the napkin and searched for words to explain why she ran, why she came back. What was there to say?

Rita broke the silence. "Your clothes need washing."

"I couldn't leave you," Angel said. "I couldn't kill anyone else. I told my mother . . ." She gritted her teeth to keep a moan from escaping. "I'm the reason that—" She had to stop.

Rita slid her hand across the table, took hold of Angel's wrist. "Not now," she said. "Later we'll talk about whatever *that* is. Right now you need to know something. You listening?"

Angel couldn't look at her but she nodded.

"You didn't kill anybody. This Scotty? What he does, he does from his own ugliness. You're not like him. You have a decent life to live. I care about you because I've gotten to know you. I see how brave you are. You came back because you have a conscience. I'd be proud if Jessie grew up to be like you."

Rita came around the table, held her, and smoothed her hair until the girl's storm passed.

THE NEXT MORNING ANGEL AND RITA GOT ANOTHER RIDE in a cruiser, this time to the school building. Angel could not keep from scanning for any moving vehicle, straining to see inside every open door and empty garage. She made herself walk, not run, from the car to the building.

While Rita prepared the tables for morning snack, Angel began walking the inside perimeter, opening every closed door, memorizing every escape route. On a high shelf above the coat hooks in the front hall she found a stocking cap and a baggy sweater. If she put them on, it could be like a disguise. Might give her a couple of extra seconds if Scotty rushed in. No. They probably belonged to one of the children.

In the kitchen, along with an exit to the back outdoor area, there was a padlocked door beside the refrigerator. A pantry? Canned goods? Tools? Interesting. Might have supplies she could use in an emergency. Wouldn't there be an extra key somewhere close? She felt around the rims of the cabinets, went through drawers beneath the counters. The ones close to the sink held silverware, cooking utensils, candles, and dish towels. The thin one beneath the cutting board was locked. She thought it probably held knives and anything else that would be dangerous for the children to handle. Next to it, beside the stove, the remaining drawer had a tangled mess of tape, twine, ribbons, screws, wires, glue tubes . . . and a ring that held fifteen or twenty keys.

She checked to make sure neither Rita nor LaDonna was watching. No key seemed to fit the knife drawer, but one of the rounded brass-colored keys fit the padlock. She glanced around again. Still okay, so she popped the lock and opened the door just a crack, knowing she'd explore more thoroughly later. Surprise. Stairs. Going up. There were two copies of this key. Angel slid one off the ring and put it in her pocket.

In the bathroom, trying to get her breathing right, she reminded herself that Scotty wouldn't come inside here. Way too many eyes. Though she believed this was true, it was still hard to calm down. For the first time she looked forward to the children's arrival, knowing that they would distract her.

Angel may have already been a little distracted, because she'd missed the rolling Suburban that kept her in sight from Rita's to the school.

AT THE SHARING CIRCLE, Angel sat beside Jessie. Norma sat directly across, wedged between Rita and LaDonna. A girl Angel hadn't met started off, holding the cork from a wine bottle. "I found this yesterday and it floats when you put it in water." Many of the children hadn't seen a cork before and were eager to touch it.

After LaDonna it was Norma's turn and she showed a folded magazine picture of a large white adobe house on cliffs overlooking a red rock canyon. "This is where my real father lives," she said, "and he wants me to come stay with him and ride horses every day." The rest of the children listened patiently but didn't look at Norma or appear to believe her story.

At Angel's turn she showed the single earring she carried. "My mom gave this to me. I don't know what it's made of." She pulled her earlobe and put the hooked end through the pierced hole, then took it out and passed it around. Most of the girls examined it carefully as if they were imagining jewelry they could wear when they grew up. The boys simply passed it along, except for one who made everyone laugh when he tried to stick it in his nose. During the circle time Norma held on to LaDonna's arm and did not look at Angel.

The next activity was movement, jumping rope. The room had enough space for two ropes whirling at the same time, two lines of children taking turns to see how long they could jump without missing. Rita and Angel kept one rope going. Norma stayed in LaDonna's group. *Down in Mississippi where the green grass grows . . .* Angel wondered if she jumped rope to these rhymes when she was younger. She didn't think so.

At free time Angel went to a table with the checkerboard. Norma went to the block area and built towers that she quickly knocked over. The other children played in clusters of two or three and ignored them both. At lunch Angel and Norma sat at separate tables.

During nap time Angel asked Rita, "What's the matter with Norma?"

"Her home's pretty unstable. She's lived with aunts and friends of the family when her dad's acting too crazy or her mom's at the shelter. It's very hard on her when someone she likes pulls a no-show, and we were both gone yesterday. LaDonna said Norma fought with the other children morning and afternoon. So today, even though we're here, she doesn't trust us. We might vanish again and, one more time, she'd have to feel sad and abandoned. Probably thinks, better for her to drop us. Less hurt."

Disappointed. Angel could understand that. How many times did Angel hope her mother would get an apartment, just the two of them? How many birthdays did she watch her mom drool over some guy and completely ignore her own daughter? How many times did her mom forget even a simple present? And Christmas? The guy would get a glitzy watch, something nice, and Angel would get a pack of barrettes and some fancy hairspray that her mom would start using in a couple of days.

After nap Angel managed to stand or sit near Norma a few times but neither spoke. Norma glanced at Angel only when she was busy with something else and could not catch her eye.

THAT EVENING TJ INTERRUPTED THEIR DINNER.

"I can't keep this twenty-four-hour thing going; we don't have the people or the budget." He took his hat off as if in apology.

"I appreciate what you've already done, and Vincente'll be back sometime tonight or tomorrow," Rita said. "What's the best way to get hold of you if we need help quick?"

"You got my personal cell number and I programmed it in one of our confiscated phones I'm giving the girl." He nodded toward Angel. "Got an hour's worth of minutes if she needs help." He handed a small black cell phone and a plug-in charger to Angel. "Keep the batteries full up. Press this to call. I'm speed dial 1, Goot's 2."

"I got Goot's cell?" Rita asked.

"Same as mine with a four at the end instead of a three."

Rita put the number in her phone's list as he continued talking.

"I still need this girl's name for my report and I need her story. The feds put a Level Two all-points on this guy"—he checked his pocket notepad—"Kramer. Darrell Scott Kramer. Fire east of Cathedral on the federal land at the edge of Joshua Tree Park. Endangered animal carcasses in the rubble. Probably substances, too. Interstate violations. ATF's part of it so there may be weapons in the mix. They only tell us enough to catch the guy. Not enough to ask the right questions once we've got him. They get to do that."

Angel's stomach had started to rumble. It sounded like people were taking Scotty seriously. It was too good to be true.

17

I need to ask you some questions," TJ said to Angel.

"Can it wait till after we finish eating?" Rita asked.

"Sorry," TJ said, "I'm out of time and me and Goot're supposed to do surveillance. Brawley's got some gangs percolating and it could spill north to you guys and Shell Beach. Good night to stay off the streets for a bunch of reasons."

He pulled a chair to him and straddled it, resting his notepad on the back. "I still don't know your name," he said.

"Angela Ann Dailey."

Rita raised her eyebrows. News to her, too.

"How long you known this Kramer?"

Angel told him about her mom meeting Scotty for the first time in Cabazon. Told about driving out into the desert and living in the trailer. Told about Scotty trapping, stealing and selling guns. Told him Scotty did drugs.

"First time I saw you you said he killed your mother?" TJ had stopped writing and looked at her.

If Angel admitted she didn't have a mother anymore would he send somebody to take her away? "What's going to happen if I tell you?" she asked.

Now TJ was surprised. "What do you mean? We'll check it out. That's our job."

"What'll happen to me?"

"I don't get it," he said. "You mean will Kramer keep coming after you?"

Angel felt her legs pushing her chair back, away from the table. Automatic reaction: run.

Rita picked up on the girl's motion. "Whoa. Hang on a minute. Are you asking can you keep staying here with me? You want to know if they'll take you away?"

TJ was looking back and forth between the two of them, impatient. "Hey, could you guys do this later? I got to split. Did you witness a murder?"

Angel put her hands on her thighs to relax them for a moment. She shook her head.

TJ, exasperated now: "So how do you know he killed your mother?"

"I found her grave," Angel said, "dug up her arm. Saw where he'd taken her rings."

Nobody moved.

TJ broke the spell. "When are you talking?"

"A few days ago," Angel said, her voice rough, hoarse. Angel could feel Rita looking at her.

TJ stood. "I'm sorry to hear that," he said. He stopped before he got to the front door. "We'll find this guy."

AFTER HE WAS GONE, Angel still felt hopeless. "He doesn't believe me, does he?"

Rita shrugged.

They exchanged cell numbers. If they were separated when trouble started, at least maybe they could send a warning.

"Matteo hasn't showed up yet, right?" Angel asked.

Rita took a deep breath, shook her head.

"Should we have told TJ about that?"

"That's Ramón's decision. He pretty much takes care of the Gomez family. They don't have cards. If we report Matteo, then Abuela and Tío might be sent back to Michoacán."

"You and Vincente got cards, right?"

"We were born here."

"Momo?"

"Same thing."

"Ramón and Carmen?"

"I think they got citizenship."

While they were doing the dinner dishes, Rita asked Angel if she had any way to prove Scotty killed her mother. Angel thought about that. And thought about that. And thought about that. There must be a way.

An hour later, neither Rita nor Angel was awake to see the

man in the old Suburban make a phone call from his parking spot at the corner of the block. Didn't hear his car start or see it crawl slowly down their street and turn right toward the highway and Cathedral City.

NEXT MORNING, Angel didn't feel like breakfast. She'd had trouble sleeping after her talk with TJ. Like she was in a tunnel. One end, Scotty, the other, foster care. Every hour brought her closer to the unfaceable.

She borrowed a pair of Rita's old jeans and rolled up the long legs. Good for traveling. At night they could work like those pajamas with feet. In spite of the heat she knew midday would bring, she tied Carmen's sweatshirt around her waist. This could be the day she'd have to run for her life and she was determined to have a fighting chance.

She made herself stay calm on the sidewalk from Rita's car to the school door. Inside, she rubbed the perspiration from her neck and forehead and went about checking the doors again. Maybe it was foolish but she wanted the outside ones unlocked. Scotty could kick in a locked one, but she couldn't break through a locked door to run out. When she examined the windows she undid the latches in the boys' bathroom and the vestibule. Call it a premonition, call it whatever you want, she was spooked and she knew it.

Before sharing circle started she found Norma burrowing in the play clothes. She waited until the girl pulled out a green cap and smelled it. Norma frowned when she saw who was standing beside her.

"I wanted to say I'm sorry for not being here," Angel began.

"I don't care," Norma said. "I don't like you."

"I don't blame you for being mad," Angel said.

"Go away." Norma threw the cap on the floor and resumed digging.

"I don't want to go away, because I like you and I'm sorry I hurt your feelings."

Norma reached behind herself with one hand and flipped Angel the bird.

Angel was shocked but it was kind of funny, too. "What are you looking for?" she asked.

Norma ignored her.

"I need a hat, too. Could you find me a blue one?" Angel asked.

"No," Norma said, not looking up.

Angel didn't move away. Quietly watched Norma search.

"What you want a hat for?" Norma asked, after a minute of tossing more and more clothes out of the box. But before Angel could answer, Norma changed her mind. "I don't care," she said, coming up finally with a multicolored scarf that she wrapped around her neck.

"You look good in scarves," Angel said, but she was speaking to Norma's back as the girl made straight for LaDonna and held on to her arm until sharing circle began.

A thin boy next to Angel held a Sucrets box in front of him as he sat. Since he was so obvious, Rita started with him. "Tell everybody your name again and what you brought for today."

106

"Primo," the boy said, "and I found this at home." He opened the box.

Angel shrieked and scooted backward. She was only dimly aware of the class pandemonium that followed as she began corralling her own panic. Embarrassing. It was only a wolf spider. She'd even made friends with a few during the evenings she'd slept outside the trailer, but she knew why she'd reacted. Watching for Scotty had made her like a snare, set to spring at the slightest pressure. Within a minute the spider was back in the box and Rita and LaDonna had restored order.

"Well, that was certainly exciting, Primo," Rita said. "Will you promise to tell me the next time you bring a pet to school?"

"He's not a pet," Primo said, his dark eyes gleaming.

Rita looked at him until he nodded, then shifted to the next person. "Angel, how about you?"

Angel smiled, thinking how close she'd come to sharing a pee stain. She reached in her pocket and pulled out the folded five-dollar bill. "This is what my mom called 'mad money.' I'm not sure where that name came from but it was like for an emergency. Like if you got in trouble and had to buy something."

"What kind of trouble?" This from the spider boy.

Angel glanced to Rita for help, but she sat patiently waiting.

"Um, well, like if your car broke and you had to get somebody to fix it," Angel said, knowing this was a stupid example.

"You don't got no car," Norma said.

The other kids ignored her, probably used to her vendettas.

"Or if you went someplace and got hungry, you could get something to eat," Angel amended, wishing she'd thought of that first.

"What do you think you could buy for five dollars?" Rita asked, and quickly added, "Not you, Angel."

"An ice cream!" a girl with heaps of curly brown ringlets said, grinning at the thought.

"Good," Rita said. "Would you have any money left over?"

The girl shrugged.

"An ice cream would be fun," Rita agreed, "but all that sugar's not good for some people. What could you buy if you wanted something healthy?"

"An orange?" Spider Boy suggested.

"That's healthy," Rita agreed. "Would you have any money left over if you paid for an orange with a five-dollar bill?"

"I'm pretty sure," the girl with ringlets said.

"Teresa's right," LaDonna chipped in. "I bought an orange yesterday at StopShop for less than a dollar."

Angel got it. Head Start. It wasn't just talking and playing. Rita and LaDonna were using these activities to teach the kids about numbers and healthy eating and thinking, all sorts of things, really. That was cool.

At movement time the jump ropes were brought out again, Angel supposed, so that the kids could get better at things they worked on the day before. Again, Norma stayed with LaDonna's group.

At free play time Rita asked the children, "Who can teach

the big girl how to play Candyland?" Everybody looked at
Norma. Norma made a face and walked to the blocks area.

"I could," Spider Boy said.

"Yeah," Angel said, "that's the least you could do."

The boy grinned and rubbed the pocket with the Sucrets
box.

As soon as they started, Angel was surprised. She actually
had fun. The boy, Primo, was a cute little guy and a pretty
sharp game-player.

At lunch an unexpected outside noise froze Angel mid-bite.

"Garbage guy," LaDonna explained.

Angel felt a momentary relief but knew this was another
reminder not to get careless, not to mess around and miss a
warning sign that could save her. At nap time she stayed by the
kitchen door to the outside. During the rest of the afternoon
Angel lost track of school activities, instead paying attention
to every unusual sound, every shadow that showed through
the windows.

The parents coming in to pick up their children at the end
of the day made her more nervous. Was he out there waiting?
She left the main room and watched from behind a screen in
the kitchen, waiting for the process to be over. After the last
child was gone, she swept while Jessie looked at picture books
and Rita called TJ for an escort home.

ON THE SHORT TRIP, Angel huddled in the corner of the
Toyota's rear seat, nervous and vigilant. At Rita's, Angel was out
and across the yard in an instant, scared of being seen. She

threw open the front door—screamed. A lone man, arms out-stretched, back to the door, had herded Rita's children to the couch. He turned just as Angel flew at him.

Angel couldn't hear his words but she heard her own. "Vincente!"

He caught her and kept her from knocking him over.

"What's the matter with you?" He was gasping for breath and the children had started crying.

"Cente! Angel! What's going on?" Rita stood wide-eyed, just inside the front door.

Angel couldn't explain. Her own fright and rage had been too awful.

Vincente pushed Angel aside.

Rita walked toward them, softly shushing the children and opening her arms to hug Vincente. "Where's your truck, honey? We didn't know you were home."

"Why didn't you tell me about the guy after you?" Vincente asked, irritated, holding Rita at arm's length. "Kids said the sheriff's been staying here."

Angel could see hurt as well as anger in his face as she stepped away. Okay, not Scotty, but her heart continued to race, ignoring the relief she felt.

Rita lowered her eyes, lowered her voice. "I'm sorry, *mi 'sposa*," she said. "I knew you would be mad. Real mad. But what would you have done if I'd called? Dropped the job. Quit and come home, right? From where? Utah? Arizona? TJ was already helping. And we need the money. There was nothing you could do 'cept worry. Right?"

"Nobody's gonna hurt you!" Vincente said, his eyes brimming with emotion. "Not gonna happen. Not never."

"You're right. I know that," Rita said, her arms out, peacemaking. "And look, *querido*, we're all here and we're okay, and you'll protect us now."

Angel could see Vincente's muscular upper body continuing to expand and contract with each breath. Even Scotty wouldn't want to face him. But Scotty wouldn't have to. He'd do his damage from cover. Angel's head throbbed and, now that she noticed, her whole body ached. She headed for the bathroom and locked the door.

She couldn't stay in this house. Could not. She'd promised, but she wouldn't do it. This whole day she'd felt like a target, like one of those milk bottles in a carnival booth. With enough throws, anyone eventually hits one and tumbles the stack. Being in this house would give Scotty enough throws.

When she sat on the edge of the tub her pants felt sticky. Perfect. Her period had started. Searching the towel closet and drawer for napkins gave her a momentary break from her predicament until a knock on the bathroom door startled her and she dropped the box she was holding.

"I got to go." Jessie's voice.

Angel guessed the recent events had scared the pee out of her. She put the supplies away and let Jessie in.

WHEN JESSIE AND ANGEL FINISHED, they returned to the living room to find everyone on the couch. Vincente held Rita, the other two kids on their laps.

"Group hug," Rita explained.

Angel waited till she got close. "I know what I said, but I can't stay here."

The kids glanced at her and burrowed their faces in their parents' arms. Vincente watched her but didn't speak. He wouldn't really know what she was referring to.

"This is the only place you're safe," Rita said, voice still soft as if she, too, was exhausted by recent events.

"No, this is the only place *you're* safe," Angel countered. "Vincente and TJ can keep Scotty out of here, but all Scotty has to do is park where he can see the house and he'll know where I am all the time. He can wait till I make a mistake."

"No, honey," Rita said. "We won't let him."

"You don't get it," Angel said, not sure she really understood, herself. "I'm like in jail. No, I'm penned up, like the Gomez animals. Waiting around for Scotty to come and get me."

"If you run he'll find you for sure," Rita said. "We've talked about this. You leave, he might try to make us tell where you went."

"Not gonna happen," Vincente said. "We should talk about this later?" he asked, nodding toward the children.

"I've been crazy scared all day," Angel said, "and I'll feel the same way here tonight. I'll be near, uh, like close enough to hear, but I have to find my own spot. Where I feel right. Where he can't corner me." Again she had water at the edge of her eyes. "Please. I have to."

"And tomorrow?" Rita asked.

Angel knew what she meant. "I have to come and go on my own," Angel said.

"You'll let me and Vincente know where you are?" Rita narrowed her eyes, clearly thinking this was a bad idea.

"I promise," Angel said.

"And tomorrow?" Rita asked again.

Angel had an impulse to cross her heart, silly when she thought about it. "I'll be there," she said. "School." She hoped that was true.

18

Angel looked for the gym bag she'd found in the Dumpster a couple of days ago but couldn't find it, guessed she dropped it when Scotty drove in. Instead she made a travel pack out of three plastic grocery bags. She jammed in a few extra clothes, some pads, tooth stuff, hairbrush, the screwdriver she'd found a few days before, the phone charger, and, last, a green liter soda bottle she'd filled with water.

While the older kids went to their room to do homework, Rita prepared dinner with Jessie's help. Angel sat in the living room on the love seat, Vincente nearby on the couch. She would leave after the meal but she needed to think about where to stay.

"I'm not exactly blaming you, but you're a load of trouble," Vincente said, cutting his eyes toward her. "I get it. We're stuck with you, but if Rita or any of my kids get hurt, you and me got a problem. Know what I mean?"

Angel knew. Better than Vincente did. She had come to know that his family was actually in more danger if she ran, but she didn't tell him that. "I'm sorry," she said, not able to look at him. "You know about the Gomez family? Matteo?"

"I do now," he said, shaking his head.

"I didn't mean to," she said. "I was just running."

He kept shaking his head as if he couldn't quite believe the extent of the bad fortune this girl brought.

Angel spoke her idea before she even realized she was thinking it. "I should kill myself." Ugly, but she meant it. That would solve everything.

That got Vincente's attention. "No. Hell, no. That's . . . a big mistake!"

Angel continued to avoid looking at him.

"Rita would never forgive herself. Or me for that matter," he said, turning, facing her squarely. "The kids would be wrecked . . . Bad example. Your life gets super tough? Suicide. Real bad example." He leaned over and backhand slapped Angel on the knee. "Don't even think it. Bad as it is, we'll figure it out."

Another gun. For a number of reasons. That's what Angel needed. Kill Scotty. And if she couldn't? If she missed? Kill herself so he couldn't have her.

"Forget about it." Rita was standing in the doorway between the living room and the kitchen.

Angel could feel the heat from her stare.

"I mean it. I never want to hear that word again. Ever. For the rest of our long life." Rita gave Angel the stern look for a few seconds more, then turned and went back in the kitchen.

Oh. Angel had thought Rita somehow knew about the gun idea, but it was "suicide." That's what she heard. So. Did Vincente have a pistol she could steal?

"You want an idea?" Vincente said.

She barely heard him. "Do you fish? Hunt?" she asked.

"Yeah," he said, dismissing the question. "You want an idea?"

"Where do you even hunt around here?" she asked, inching her way toward her goal.

"Scrub, ridges," he answered, "but we're not going hunting, so listen up."

"Can I see your stuff?" she asked. "Like a compass? You use binocs or . . . or you got a scope on your gun?"

His eyebrows crinkled and she could see his puzzlement. She saw she was going too fast, maybe even in the wrong direction. He might not have a gun or, if he did, he might not keep a pistol and his rifle in the same place. Dinner. During dinner she'd excuse herself to the bathroom and search their bedroom instead. A pistol, if he owned one, would probably be near the ceiling on a closet shelf.

"Don't be a goofball." His confusion had morphed to anger. "You want a suggestion or not?"

She didn't. "Sure," she said.

"What about my tractor?"

It was her turn to be puzzled. "Tractor?"

"My truck. My truck cab has a sleeping cabin behind it. Can't tell a person's in there from the outside. Got a bed. Reading light. Cooler. Runs on battery. It's parked a block over. You're not going to find a place better'n that."

Wow. That was a good idea. Maybe an amazing idea. Angel couldn't have been more surprised.

"You and me, sneak out after dinner. Take a look at it. You don't like it, no big deal," Vincente said, rising. "I'm gonna set the table." He left Angel alone to consider it.

She did. Along with considering whether their bedroom had more than one closet.

THE TRUCK CAB WAS ACTUALLY COZY. And safe. And for the first time in weeks, Angel got a good night's sleep. And toward morning, a dream.

She is alone, walking, way out in the desert. She begins to understand she is following something or someone, tracking actually, and she begins to pay attention to the ground in front of her. The tracks, depressions in the sand, are blurred, and she cannot tell whether they're made by an animal or a person. She follows them along a dry wash, past a smoke tree, and then the prints begin climbing a ridge. She understands she will be able to see what she is following when she reaches the top and she begins to feel more and more anxious. Her sense of danger gets unbearable near the crest.

She awoke to complete darkness inside the sleeping compartment, her heart thumping like she'd been running. She lay still, going back over the dream, wondering why it had been so scary. What had she thought was over the crest of the hill? Scotty? Her mother? A dead body walking? *No.* She had to stop thinking and get out of the truck. Since she'd slept in her clothes, all she had to do was crawl out of the compartment and peek through the windshield to see whether the coast was clear.

The night before, she'd searched Rita and Vincente's bedroom. Not a wooden box. A thick canvas bag with a drawstring. In his closet, on the highest shelf under a blanket, the first place she'd looked. Two pistols, each wrapped in an oily handkerchief. One had a long thin barrel and looked weird, almost like a squirt gun. The heavier one had a short barrel and round cylinder that held larger bullets. She'd shot that kind before at the trailer. She replaced the canvas bag, leaving the weird pistol in it, and hid the other gun behind the towels in the bathroom closet.

So now, today, she needed time to search for the bullets. She'd have to be careful since Vincente would probably be home for the weekend. She was pretty sure he stored the bullets fairly near the gun; close enough to grab if there was trouble. She bet they were in the nightstand by his pillow or in his top dresser drawer where he probably kept his underwear. She knew a thing or two about this. Since ten or eleven she'd been searching through the men's belongings wherever her mom stayed. Like a treasure hunt. Finders keepers.

ANGEL OPENED RITA'S FRONT DOOR to the cheerful buzz of children. Their mood had been quiet and watchful since the night they'd been sent to friends' houses for safety. This morning they were teasing, arguing, chattering. Either they were glad it was the weekend or something good had happened.

Angel could hear Vincente laughing in the kitchen. When she walked in for breakfast Rita and Vincente were standing by the sink, his arms around her waist.

"What?" Angel said, coming to the table.

Rita blushed and turned out of his grasp. "TJ called," she said. "Cops picked him up. Outside a pawnshop in south Palm Springs. Handed him over to the feds."

"Scotty?" Angel could hardly believe it.

"Scotty. You can stop worrying." Rita went to her side, hugged her, swung her around, and set her down. "Free . . . You should celebrate! We should celebrate. What would you like?"

Angel was at a loss. She knew she should be happy but really, she was stunned. Safe? Free? It was unbelievable. If that were true, what would she like to do? A rush of sadness invaded. Had her mother, her poor dumb dead mother, ever asked her how she would like to celebrate? Angel turned away quickly to keep Rita and Vincente from seeing her eyes. "I don't know." It came out like a croak. "Uh, what could we do?"

"Go to that place in La Quinta for a seafood dinner?" This from Vincente.

"*Aye, cabrón*," Rita teased, "you always think with your stomach."

"Not always," Vincente teased back, giving Rita a look that

Angel would have understood immediately if she'd been facing them.

"Okay, um, that's an idea but with the kids eating, you'd have to sell the truck," Rita said, smiling and shaking her head.

"Yeah, pretty 'spensive," Vincente agreed. "How about that all-you-can-eat place? Kids free there?"

Angel quickly realized she didn't want to cost them any more money. "We could eat an early dinner here, and after you could take me to the club, maybe an ice cream, and we could walk along the water and you could show me places you like." Her face was dry now, and composed. She turned and faced them, smiling. "Going for a walk without looking over my back all the time."

The kids scurried out the door to play with neighborhood friends and Angel followed soon after, hoping to give Rita and Vincente some time alone together. Without having to worry about being jumped, she liked being outdoors again, the sunshine, the desert landscape, the stubborn plants. The land was rough but it wasn't barren like she'd first thought.

Giving the area a slow once-over, she spotted the house with the high platform that she and Rita had climbed. Now that she was looking, she realized several houses had a platform like that, over a carport, or on the corner of the house with the best view. That brought Scotty to mind again. Where had he parked a couple of nights ago? Had he left a cigarette butt or anything? She pictured where Vincente had parked his truck when she'd first arrived and imagined where the ruts would be that she'd seen from the rooftop. Walking slowly, examining the west side of the street, sure enough, Angel easily found the furrows leading back toward the highway.

After several steps, she noticed that she was looking at tire tracks. There should be at least two sets: Goot's cruiser when he drove up to check Scotty and Scotty's own, and maybe more, but in the few days Angel had lived with Rita she'd never seen any other car parked in that place. As she walked, she saw only two different prints, one a couple of inches wider than the other. The pickup was probably the wider. And she remembered. Her dream. Tracking. And then something else. Something big. She couldn't believe she'd thought of it.

Rita had asked her if there was any way she could prove Scotty had killed her mother . . . His tracks? His tire prints leading to her grave? Had it rained? No. And these were his truck's tire prints! A sheriff could make some kind of copy and compare them with the tire prints leading north from the ruined trailer. And find where her mother had been buried . . . and if he'd moved her, where he'd gone, probably up closer to those jagged ridges.

Got you.

THAT SAME AFTERNOON, waiting for TJ to respond to Rita's call about the tire tracks, Angel wondered for the first time where Norma lived, wondered whether Norma would like to go for a walk. Salt Shores was such a strange mix between an old-fashioned village and a ghost town. Exploring it reminded her of hunting for arrowheads like she'd done one time with her mother and Scotty. If you looked closely, you never knew what you might find.

Through Rita's front window, Angel saw the cruiser arrive, saw TJ get out and reach back inside for his hat. She lost sight of him as he walked to the door. The kids were off playing with friends and Vincente was in the love seat watching some ball game on TV. Angel sat with Rita on the couch, holding pencil and paper, making a list of words for a game she was going to play with the children. Angel knew Rita was nervous. She'd already bitten the erasers off two pencils.

Angel was ready, but TJ's knock startled everybody else. Vincente muted the TV and Rita set her things aside while Angel let TJ in. He was taller than she'd remembered. Her head was level with his adam's apple.

"Thanks . . . ," she said, faltering. Figuring out this tire thing had given her some confidence, but she seemed to lose it in TJ's presence.

TJ looked past her. "Rita, Vincente," he said, standing just inside the front door. "You had something you wanted to tell me?"

Angel could sense Vincente and Rita looking at her. She'd told them she had to talk to TJ. She hadn't told them what this was about. "Uh, I thought of something," Angel began.

TJ breathed through his nose, his face blank, waiting.

"Okay, uh, you want to prove Scotty killed my mom, get his tire prints from where Goo—" She stopped because TJ was already impatient, grimacing. Angel's stomach dipped for a second, but she started again. "You get his tire tracks where the deputy checked him out, across the road here. You take those to the burned trailer up by the Gom—" This time she was stopped by Rita's head shake and the pained expression on her face.

They aren't legal.

"I got things to do," TJ said, looking at Vincente, like he was sure another man would understand.

Angel wouldn't back off. "You said people were investigating a fire east of Cathedral City. I know that place. That's where Mom and I lived with Scotty. In a trailer at the end of some ruts. Rita can probably tell you pretty close. That's where the fire was. That's where he killed Mom and drove away and buried her. I told you. I followed him. Later, when he knew I knew, he came back to the trailer and tried to kill me, too. Burned everything to wreck the evidence."

The disdain left TJ's face while he dug in his shirt pocket for his notepad. "Okay, give it to me," he said, "but I don't know what'll happen. We just got your word. No body or nothing."

19

TJ's visit had put a damper on Saturday evening. Remembering about Angel finding her mother's fresh grave was just too gruesome. They rushed through a tamale dinner and afterward made popcorn, watched a TV movie, and went to bed early.

Sunday morning the whole family took a long walk south from the club, following the water's edge. Angel asked about the white crunchy stuff that they kept stepping on. Picking up a handful, she examined delicate hollow shells that looked like beads. Barnacle shells, Vincente told her. Zillions of them, joining the dead drying fish and matted bird feathers that made a carpet beside the sea. "Too salty," Rita said. "No boats 'cause motors get ruined, and most fish can't survive, but the birds love it."

The kids taught Angel the funny bird names—grebes, cormorants, egrets, bitterns—but her favorites were the big white pelicans that glided five or six feet above the water's surface and crash-dived whenever they spotted a fish. Jessie found an old oar, Rita picked up a mangled pair of reading glasses with one frosty lens remaining, and Angel discovered a corroded black-and-yellow license plate that she decided to keep for a souvenir.

Back at the club, everybody had chocolate-covered ice cream cones and Vincente had a beer. That night they all fell asleep in the living room listening to a new CD that Vincente had brought home from a store in Tucson.

ANGEL AWOKE MONDAY MORNING in the tractor cab feeling more than just rested, feeling good, energetic. On the short walk to Rita's she ran her fingers through her hair. Would Rita give her a haircut? She noticed a tall, thin cactus with red blossoms. Had that been there before? The white grit, the weathered pastel houses, the tall palm trees and scrubby plants, could this place actually be beautiful? She smiled. What was the matter with her? Gas fumes from the truck?

Rita and Jessie were on the porch waiting when she walked up. Rita handed her a banana. "Breakfast," she said. "Let's get going. You can wash up at the school."

Jessie bounded ahead of them and Angel felt like holding Rita's hand as they turned the corner but she didn't.

"Another scorcher," Rita said, fanning her face. "Next couple of weeks could be in the hundreds and it's just the end of May. You know school's almost out. What you gonna do then?" she asked. "Think you might stay around here?"

Angel didn't answer but the question made her feel even better. Rita didn't hate her. Didn't resent her for all the trouble she'd caused. What would she do next, once Scotty was in prison? It seemed like a miracle. She wouldn't have to keep running. She could choose. A future.

LATER THAT MORNING AT SCHOOL, Angel was waiting for Norma in the vestibule. "Hi. You still mad at me?" she asked, offering Norma a fat red grape from the food supplies.

"You suck," Norma said, batting at the grape but missing.

"You're a grouch," Angel said, popping the grape in her own mouth.

"Hey, that's mine," Norma complained.

"You didn't want it," Angel said, kneeling down a little so she'd be more on the girl's own level. "Want me to see if I can find you another one?"

Norma turned her back like she was mad.

"Go on in," Angel said. "I'll look."

Angel picked the biggest grape she could find off the bunch reserved for morning snack and found Norma standing by the table-games shelf, pulling out one box after another. "Want to teach me Candyland today?" Angel asked, handing her the red seedless.

"Primo did," Norma said, pouty.

Angel was surprised the girl had noticed. And glad. "Want to teach me something else?"

"No," Norma said, walking away.

But at game time, Norma was shuffling through the boxes again.

Rita, observant as usual, asked, "Who would be willing to teach the big girl a new game?"

Primo's hand shot up. "Me, me."

"You did a great job showing her Candyland yesterday," Rita said, "so let's give someone else a chance."

Norma, carrying a small cardboard box, practically stomped over to the table where Angel sat. "Tic-toe," she announced, defiant, daring anyone to dispute her claim.

"That's a good one," Rita said. "Thanks. Tomorrow it can be another person's turn."

Norma frowned, sat down, dumped the contents, and shoved the O's at Angel. "I start," she said.

AT NAP TIME ANGEL SAT BESIDE RITA, watching the children, trying to remember if she had ever taken naps.

"Looks like you have a friend again," Rita said, pursing her lips.

"She told me her and her sister are going to run away. Buy their own house," Angel said. "I used to dream about the same thing."

"I know Norma's real troubled by the things she's seen at home, but she's fierce. She fights back, tries to hold her own," Rita said. "I can't understand this domestic violence thing. The wife, it's usually the wife, keeps expecting the guy's going to change or really, really hopes he's going to change, and she keeps coming back for more . . . or maybe she thinks she doesn't deserve any better. Maybe she saw it in her own home as a kid and assumes that's just the way families are. I guess I should study it, 'cause it really stumps me. I'd shoot Vincente if he pounded me in front of the kids."

Angel nodded, remembering the gun she'd hidden. That afternoon a gray-haired woman hand-delivered Rita's and LaDonna's paychecks and that evening Rita drove everyone to the huge Safeway in Indio for the month's new groceries.

TUESDAY NORMA WAS STANDING in the hall waiting for her when Angel came out of the bathroom. "Hi," Norma said, "I got new panties."

"That's nice," Angel said, laughing, "I wish I could say the same thing."

Norma stepped back and examined Angel's face.

"I'm not kidding," Angel said. "Let's do a quick tic-toe before circle starts."

Norma grinned and ran to get the game.

THE CALL CAME ON RITA'S CELL ABOUT AN HOUR LATER. Angel couldn't hear the conversation but she could tell by Rita's face that something had happened. Bad news. TJ gave Rita the details and she passed them on to Angel after she hung up.

Scotty had told the investigators he was a taxidermist living alone in a trailer near the ridges that bordered Joshua Tree Park. Said the trailer caught fire one night when he was in town drinking with friends. A couple of local businessmen corroborated his story, one a pawnshop owner, the other, a locksmith.

Scotty told them the animal carcasses they found were either roadkill he'd salvaged or taxidermy projects he hadn't started yet. Said the animals were long dead before the fire. The feds had lab guys checking that out but it would take at least a month to get the results. Scotty denied everything about drugs and said he'd kept some weapons for use in his guide service. He paid fines for burning and creating a nuisance on public land. He agreed to stay in the area if they needed to question him further. Since they didn't have any conclusive evidence, they released him.

They released him. The words made a vacuum. Angel filled it with rage. She shouldn't have expected any help. The system had always been against her. Really, there was *never* any help, was never going to be any help. She was and would be alone, and hope for anything different was a stupid waste of time. She left the kickball game without looking back and exited through the rear door. A tall century plant at the front corner of the building hid her as she scanned the block for Scotty. Mid-morning no one seemed to be outside, no cars were moving.

Okay, Angel would walk these streets and look at every vehicle. Get a sense of which ones belonged in this neighborhood, which houses looked vacant, what building or foliage could hide a pickup. In other words, get the lay of the land so she'd have an idea where Scotty could watch undetected. She turned right at the sidewalk. White house, black car; tan house, vacant; two empty lots; white house, red pickup; more vacant lots; trailer house, white Ford; and so on, turning right at each corner until she passed by Rita's and retraced her morning route to the school. Did this make any sense? It was really only a rectangle of four streets that had good access to Rita's. There weren't that many cars and trucks, a few more probably away at people's work. Well, it was a start, and the walking burned off some of the anger.

Fifty miles north her mother's killer was also walking. Heading to a Greyhound station, buying a one-way ticket to Los Angeles.

FOR THE SECOND TIME THAT MORNING, Angel stood behind the big saw-leafed plant at the corner of the school wondering what to do next. She couldn't face going inside, talking, explaining. The longer she stood there, the more tired she felt. Or maybe not tired, exactly, more like what's-the-difference. How could she possibly keep tabs on Scotty? She'd have to sit up on the roof platform with binoculars and watch every car that left Highway 86 and drove east into the town. She'd have to be sure that nobody parked along the highway and walked across the open land past StopShop to Rita's street. Watch 24/7. That's what it would take to see him coming . . . if he hadn't already driven straight here and hidden someplace, waiting for night.

The enormity of the task seeped into her, numbing as it went, until she lost the will to remain standing. Gravity pulled her to the ground and leaned her against the side wall. *She couldn't guard against Scotty.* The thought echoed in the empty halls of her mind and Angel felt herself fading away, getting smaller, disappearing.

THE NEXT THING SHE NOTICED WAS THE PHONE RINGING. In Rita's living room. She had no memory of getting there. Through the shades she could see it was dark outside. Had Rita led her home? Had someone carried her?

Vincente answered. When he hung up, he told Rita and Angel. That was TJ. Police had found Scotty's truck at a used-car lot in Indio. Sold for cash. The dealer said the seller had gone away on foot. Now nobody knew where Darrell Scott Kramer was, or what kind of vehicle he might be driving.

Had Angel sensed he was going to do that? Was that why she reacted immediately, walked the blocks, noting the cars? Like Scotty had bored into her mind, transmitted his thoughts? She could practically feel him inside her, feel his invasion. This had become a competition he needed to win, had to win. Really, the smart thing for him to do would be to leave now, go to another state, operate his business somewhere else. And he might do that later. But not now. Angel knew it in her bones. Scotty was locked on to her, the hunt, the challenge, and he wouldn't drop it. Wouldn't stop until he'd killed her. And how she knew that, she couldn't say, but she absolutely knew it. Dead certain.

Rita interrupted Angel's thinking. "Cente, you grew up with TJ. Would he be willing to make some copies of Kramer's driver's license picture, take it to the StopShop? Give us some to show?"

"Probably don't really look like him," Vincente said, dismissing the idea, catching his top lip between his teeth, clearly wishing Angel had never brought his family all this trouble.

"Better than nothing, *mi 'sposa*." Rita was using that soft voice that seemed to disarm most arguments. "Don't want him snaking around here invisible. *You* got no clue what he looks like."

"He won't . . ." Angel's voice was scratchy and she started over. "He won't come here right away. He needs to let things die down."

"Yeah, like you're the expert, right? You got him solved? That's how come you're begging around here?" Vincente, shaking his head.

"Cente! *Ya basta*. She didn't ask for this. Jessie could have this kind of trouble one of these days and you'd want *alguien a ayudarla*. Be there. Help her."

Vincente thought it over. Nodded. "I'll call him."

Angel wanted off the couch. She needed to leave. She put her fists on the cushion to lever herself up but her arms were weak. Where was her energy? She should be afraid. She should be moving. She knew it but she couldn't do it. Maybe Rita had given her a sleeping pill. Angel had seen her mom take those and turn into a zombie. She leaned over and rested her head on the arm of the sofa. That felt good.

SHE AWOKE TO AN EMPTY ROOM. As she sat up she realized her clothes were damp. *Oh, no.* But it didn't smell. Sweat. She could barely see in the dimness, shards of light from a distant streetlamp coming through the shades. She stifled an impulse to part the blinds and look out. What if he was here already? Watching. What if he wasn't but someone else was? Did he really have friends who would get involved?

Her stomach boiled. Had she eaten? She didn't think so. Maybe she was sick. Cancer. Like Goot's wife. Maybe she'd die before Scotty got to her. Her face itched and she rubbed it. She moaned and shut up immediately, afraid she'd wake someone. She couldn't stand for anyone to see her.

What could she do? Shoot herself? Where was the pistol she'd found? Couldn't she keep track of anything? She dug her fingernails into her palms for punishment. She was such a pathetic loser. She lay back down and shut her eyes. People could make themselves die. Hadn't she read that? Just stop breathing. But a sound jarred her. She froze solid, listening. It came again. A howl. A cat. Outdoors. Prowling. That did it. She had to get out of there.

The good thing about Rita's? Unlike at the Gomez place, surrounded by flat desert, Scotty couldn't cover Rita's house from one vantage point. So how would she leave? She remembered two things simultaneously: the pistol behind the towels in the bathroom, and the platform. The pistol wouldn't do her any good, because she hadn't found the bullets yet and Vincente and Rita were probably sleeping in their bedroom. But the rooftop? What if Scotty had climbed it and was already scoping the house from that corner? If he was up there, was there a blind spot he couldn't see? Where were the travel things she'd packed before? Never mind. She had to hide. She'd come back later.

Angel slipped out the back door and snuck along the side of the house away from the lookout. At the corner of the building she got on her knees and peered around. She located the high platform, scanned it thoroughly. Empty. Pretty sure. She stood and examined the street in front. No one in sight and nothing moving. She missed the cigarette butts that shouldn't have been lying on the ground under the front window.

Okay, so where could she go? On her way around the house she'd seen a play tent the kids had made out of a dark blanket over a clothesline in the backyard. That would do for tonight. It wasn't like she needed to sleep. No, she needed to think whether there was any way out of this. She collected the blanket and wrapped it around her, more for protection than for warmth. She crept forward again and sat with her back against the front corner, remembering that Scotty had gone down the other side of the house when he broke in a few nights before.

Did TJ pass her information on to the other police? She wasn't sure. Probably not if he thought they'd dismiss it as just another runaway blaming everybody but herself. Would he follow up on what she had told him about the tire prints? Maybe. But even if he did, that could take days, and if the police went after Scotty seriously then, they wouldn't know where to find him. How long did Angel have? Was Scotty out there now? Okay, back to her formula. First things first. Like Ramón had said, think!

What would Scotty do? The feds let him go. He'd sold his truck. Now he was under the radar again. If he came after her immediately, got her, killed her, he'd be the prime suspect.

He'd be wanted for kidnapping. Scotty wouldn't choose that much heat. He'd let things cool off for a while . . . three weeks? A month? That way, when Angel disappeared it would seem like maybe she'd run off. It wouldn't be like murder. She'd be just another face on a flyer.

So he'd hide out and wait. With a friend? She didn't think so. She never heard him talk about friends. She couldn't imagine he'd room with anybody. He'd stay alone or find himself another woman. Either way, at first he'd need a motel. Or buy a new trailer. How much money did he have? Scotty wasn't the saving type, but he'd have cash from selling his truck. He'd always kept his wallet chained to his jeans and maybe he had another stash buried near the trailer. How much? She had no idea. How much was a trailer? She stopped herself. Pure guessing wasn't good enough. She didn't know enough to figure this stuff out.

Okay, motel. He would want a place close to Salt Shores, but not too obvious. He could stay to the north of the sea, Indio or Coachella, but that was probably too close to home, too visible for Scotty. When she drove down here with Momo, once they'd turned south off 10 she didn't see any towns with motels. Just some dried-up settlements. The motel in Rita's town had been long closed, boarded up. She'd have to ask about Brawley.

Three weeks or a month in a motel would cost him. Angel did a quick guesstimate: last time she and her mom had to stay in a motel it had been eighty something a night. Times three weeks. That could run way over a thousand, particularly if he didn't find a new woman right away. And he'd probably meet her in a bar and wine her and dine her at first. That'd cost a little. He'd need to have a bunch of money stashed or he'd have to keep working, and Angel didn't think Scotty would take a real job. And he probably wouldn't chance getting caught at something illegal so soon. So best guess, Scotty could maybe afford to lay low for a month, not much longer.

Another thing she knew for sure: he'd get a new truck. Scotty wasn't a car kind of guy, and if he wanted to pick up a new woman he wouldn't drive a beater. He'd be tooling around in some kind of macho ride. So that'd cost megamoney. He wouldn't rent one, 'cause that would leave a trail.

Leave a trail . . . She was shocked at what she was thinking. *Hunt Scotty!*

Could she find him? In a month? Maybe. Find him and shoot him.

Angel was surprised how well she had come to know men like Scotty. She could make up a soap about his life on a moment's notice. Like where would he stay? Not too far, 'cause he'd want to keep track of whether Angel was still around Rita's. He'd stand out in tiny towns. A stranger staying too long in the only motel? People would ask questions. So he'd need a place with a little size. Okay, a pickup, a motel, maybe in Brawley, and the bar or dating scene. Could Angel find him before he found her?

Wow. Tracking Scotty. Was that even possible? What would she do if she were right? If she actually found him? Tell TJ? Maybe. Maybe not. Would she shoot?

The hum of an engine ripped her out of her concentration. Cars don't make that much noise. A pickup. Slowing and stopping in front. Angel pulled the blanket off her shoulders and crouched, ready to flee. Should she warn Rita? She tugged the phone out of her pocket.

This late at night there were no sounds, no radios or pets barking. Even the highway was quiet. Angel could hear the engine cooling, could see when the headlights were turned off. Waiting, she knew what she would do. As soon as he went around the side or up to the front door, she'd scoot over the fence and get to the empty tan house a couple of doors up nearer the main street. At least she could hide in the open garage until he left or something else happened.

The quiet continued. She was afraid he'd hear her using the phone, so she held it, waiting for the right moment, but he didn't get out. The truck door didn't open. Angel frowned. He couldn't just wait there. Way too visible. Too stupid.

Angel heard the front porch door unlatch and the screen open. Uh-oh. Vincente. And Vincente would shoot him . . . but Angel had taken his gun. His biggest pistol. And Scotty would have a cannon. She was going to get Rita's husband killed.

"Hey! You crazy?" Vincente's voice.

The pickup door opened and Angel crawled closer, as if that would do any good. Should she scream?

"I'm s'posed to knock on the door and get shot?"

That wasn't Scotty's voice. But familiar . . . Momo? Angel peeked around the corner.

"No, you s'posed to visit in the goddamn daytime, loco

boy. So I don't put a hole in you 'fore you can shake your pecker."

"Hey, I'm sorry, Uncle," Momo said, holding his hands up like he was surrendering. "I was going to nap out here till you woke up. I didn't want to cause no trouble."

"Right. I shoot you, kill your folks and Ramón with the same bullet. Use your *cabeza*, numbnuts. Call us. You know what's been happening?"

"Kinda."

"Right. So get in here before Angel whacks you with a rake. She's around here somewhere."

Momo saw her as he walked toward the door. Stopped. Surprised. Didn't know what to do.

Angel stood, only then realizing she probably looked awful. She slipped the phone back in her pocket and crossed her arms. Felt even more self-conscious. She wheeled, deciding to enter the house from the back. Indoors, Angel went directly to the bathroom and checked her face in the mirror. Her hair looked like she'd chewed it off and, in spite of being almost comatose the past day, she had dark circles under her eyes. Where did this concern about her appearance come from? Was she going to turn out like her mom?

20

I need help," Angel said, back on the couch, knees pulled up in front of her.

"Just now noticing?" Vincente said, cutting his eyes toward Momo.

Momo was sitting in a chair to her right. His arms were like she remembered: brown, strong, veins like rivers. Wearing a dirty gray sleeveless sweatshirt, stained jeans, and thick-soled black boots, he must have just left work. His hair was damp from the baseball cap that rested on his knee, and there was a dark smudge on his cheek.

"No, I mean it. I have to find Scotty."

"Know when he gets here?" Vincente clarified.

"No, find him. Before he gets here."

That left both men speechless. They were still staring at

Angel when Rita came in from the bedroom, barefoot in a long Raiders T-shirt. As soon as she saw Momo she went back to get dressed.

"I think I know what he'll do, where he'll go to wait," Angel said. "I have to find him before he finds me." She sat on the couch at the far end from Vincente and tried not to look at Momo.

"I don't think so," Vincente said, shaking off the surprise. "Pin in a haystack. Even if you found him, then what? Citizen arrest? Wise up." He stood abruptly and followed Rita into the bedroom.

Angel could feel her face flushing. Was she so stupid?

"How you gonna find him?" Momo asked.

"How much is a trailer?" Angel responded, suddenly full of questions for someone with more experience out in the world.

WHEN VINCENTE AND RITA RETURNED, Angel and Momo were on the couch with the *Imperial Valley Press* spread out between them. Momo had his finger on a picture of a truck; Angel had lined paper and one of Rita's pencils.

"'99 Ford 350, Super Duty, that's big enough to haul a trailer, but it's eighty-five hundred. He couldn't get much of a rig for less." Momo continued to run his finger down the page.

"Hey, this is crazy," Vincente said, turning to look at Rita for confirmation.

"Take it easy, Uncle," Momo said. "We're just looking. She could be right."

"I told you," Vincente said to Rita.

Angel didn't want to look up from her calculations, afraid of what she might see in Rita's eyes.

"Yeah, well, since everybody's up, how 'bout I make chilaquiles? Give these two a minute to work on things and then we can talk at the table."

When Angel glanced up, she saw Rita had hold of Vincente's arm and was pulling him into the kitchen.

"So we should check the library," Momo said. "They got computers and we can check Craigslist. Some cheaper trucks there, but no matter how you cut it, he's gotta have several thousand for nice wheels and a motel to lay low the way you're thinking."

"Will you help me find him?" Angel asked, keeping her eyes on her numbers.

Momo looked away. Angel dreaded his answer. *Everybody thinks I'm crazy.*

"Uh, I got to call Dad and Ray and Carmen," Momo said. "See if they need me up there this break. If they don't got nothing major going on I could give you a couple of days."

THE ATMOSPHERE AT THE KITCHEN TABLE FELT AWFUL. Angel could tell she and her problems were blowing this home apart but she didn't know what else to do. Shame or no shame, she had to keep fighting. Maybe Vincente was right. First, so drained she could hardly move, a few hours later talking about fighting. Manic. Again the urge to run, but before she could move, Vincente reached across the table and grabbed her shoulder. Everybody jumped up, not sure what would happen next.

"The hell's it take to knock some sense in you?" He was practically yelling. "I got short runs starting today. I can't be watchdoggin' while you and SuperMex here get yourselves killed."

Rita had hold of his shirtsleeve. "Cente, Cente! *Cálmate.* She's right, Vin. He won't do nothing right now. Hole up, that's all. And I got Goot and TJ looking out for us. You work. That's what's got to happen."

Angel could see the rage in Vincente's face starting to soften. Momo was practically vibrating beside her, hands clenched.

Rita sat and dragged Vincente back into his chair. "She'll do what she has to," Rita said, looking at Angel. "You tell her no but it don't work like that. *Mira. Es lo que tiene que hacer. Es* more than reason."

Angel looked to Momo for meaning.

"You do what you got to do," he said.

Angel looked back to Vincente. Seemed like he was still seething. He pointed at Angel like she was the one who was ruining everything. He moved his hand to point at Momo.

"Okay, *vato.* You stick your dick in this, it's on you. My family gets hurt—" He stormed out of the room, the sentence dangling like a noose.

The room became so quiet Angel could hear the wall clock. She wondered if she really understood what she was doing, what consequences it could have, but it didn't matter. She was going to look for Scotty even if she had to do it alone. Even if it killed her.

21

The front door closing woke Angel out of a sound sleep. Morning light filtered through the shades. The living room was empty but she could hear people in the kitchen. She cleaned up in the bathroom and went to see what was going on. Momo and Rita were talking over coffee.

"Vincente probably won't be back till after dark," Rita told her. "Momo's got some business to take care of and you're going to school with me and Jessie. He'll pick you up this afternoon."

Momo nodded at her, confirming.

Angel didn't argue.

At school, she helped Rita get the tables ready. When she went to the kitchen for the napkins, she remembered the padlock, felt for the key in her pocket. "Where's the door go to?"

Rita looked where Angel was looking. "Attic," she said. "Before, when this was a church, I think they stored stuff up there. Pretty sure it's empty now."

Empty!

Angel began sifting through cupboards to find towels and tablecloths she could take upstairs for bedding, but her search was interrupted by the children's arrival. Norma found her immediately.

"Brought you something," Norma said, grinning but shy, holding the bottom of her skirt.

"What?"

"This," Norma said, and dropped a raisin in Angel's hand. "It's like a baby grape, only it don't squish up. You can put it in your pocket."

"Hey, thanks." Angel tucked it down by the five-dollar bill. "I have something to tell you."

Norma looked up at her, very pleased.

"I . . . I may not be here every day or I may leave early some days. I got to do some stuff."

The smile left Norma's face. "What stuff?"

Angel wasn't sure what to say, realizing too late she should have asked Rita about this conversation. "I have to find somebody. Pretty quick."

"Why?"

"Uh"—Angel hoped this was okay—"you know there are some bad guys out in the world, right?"

Norma gave an exaggerated nod. "Real bad," she said. "Bad bad."

"Yeah, well . . . one of those guys from where I used to live is chasing me . . . and I have to find him first . . . so he can't hurt me." Angel looked away and shook her head. That was probably way more than the little girl needed to know.

"I seen bad guys," Norma said, starting to pick her nose. She thought a moment. "I'll help. What's he look like?"

"You don't need to hel—" Angel stopped because Norma's face was clouding over. "Okay," she amended. "It's a guy, right?"

Norma nodded, relieved, and screwed her face into a super-concentration mode.

"He's an older guy."

"White hair?" Norma was into this.

"No, not that old. Okay, you know what a country-western singer looks like? A guy?"

Norma thought for a moment. "On TV?"

"Yeah, cap or cowboy hat, uh, blondish hair, darker than mine, not too long. Mustache. Slim. Button shirt, sleeves rolled up."

"Long pants?"

Angel had to hold her face set. In spite of how serious this was, Norma was cracking her up. "Yeah, jeans. Usually black jeans."

"Mean?" Norma asked.

"Yes," Angel said, "very, very mean. And if you ever see him, don't let him know. Be real cool, right."

"I am cool," Norma said. "Like popsicles."

Angel didn't know what to say to that, but fortunately Rita called everybody to circle.

MOMO PICKED HER UP DURING NAP TIME. Angel had fluffed her hair and scrubbed her face so her cheeks had some blush. She wore one of Rita's light cotton sweater tops and the cargo pants/running shoes again. Momo had told her: "We're gonna be driving around places, maybe asking questions. We gotta look right. Like we're shopping or something. Like we're . . . you know, together. I'll say I'm trying to find my friend and you'll, like, be my, um, my sister, maybe. Or a friend. We got to be casual like we know what we're doing."

Momo looked her over as she climbed in.

She could feel her face coloring. Didn't look at him. "Can we go by the StopShop first?"

"You need something?"

That hadn't occurred to Angel. She ran a mental checklist on the contents of the small purse Rita had loaned her. Maybe more pads, but she wouldn't buy those when she could borrow them. Borrow them. Right. That made her smile.

"What?"

"Oh, uh, I told this girl about Scotty today. She wanted to help. Made me think I should tell StopShop too. Tell them be careful if there's a guy asking about me. Tell them call the police after he leaves."

"Good idea." He rested his elbow on the open window ledge.

Angel remembered that from the first day she met him.

"Got some news," he said.

"What?"

"Saw TJ. He said tell Rita and you that Cathedral police had a guy matches Scotty's description on the morning bus to L.A. yesterday. He's outta here. You can stop worrying."

That didn't ease Angel's mind. "He's going to buy a truck where it's harder to trace," she said.

Momo nodded. Probably thought she was totally paranoid. She wasn't. She just knew Scotty.

Angel knew him even better than she thought. Yesterday, he had slipped off the L.A.-bound bus unnoticed during the brief stop in Ontario, about eighty miles from where he'd boarded. At a convenience store, he picked up a truck shopper magazine. Hours later he struck a phone deal with a private party for a dark green four-wheel drive Ford 350 with the big diesel. Today, before he headed back to the Salton area in his new ride, he had a couple of errands: an army surplus store for two pairs of handcuffs, a hardware store for eyebolts and locking carabiners that would attach the cuffs to the passenger side door and floor plate.

"So you want to cruise this afternoon?" Momo asked. "Check out motels? Get a feel for Brawley. Places where guys meet women. Clubs, music, dancing. Get a line on those."

"Who'd know that?"

"Find a guy looks like me. Ask him."

Angel didn't get it, then she did. Scowled at him.

"Hey, just jokin'. I don't do that."

Angel couldn't help herself. "You already got a girlfriend?"

"Not yet. You applying? I'm too old for you."

"Stop the car."

"What?"

"Stop the goddamn car!" Angel was opening the truck door, getting ready to jump.

"Hey!" Momo stood on the brakes, which slung the heavy door open. Angel went out with it, hanging on as best she could till it slid out of her hands and she tumbled to the road.

Momo skidded to a stop, rammed it in park, and was out his door running.

By the time he reached her, she was on her feet, pants torn, palms and knees bleeding, embarrassed, rubbing a knot on her forehead, eyes wet with pain. When he got close she kicked at him. "Don't you ever . . . Never! You never talk to me—" She didn't have enough breath to keep her words going. "I don't need you." She hobbled away in the direction of the Stop-Shop.

WHEN SHE WALKED OUT OF THE STORE, rubbing her hands on paper towels from the restroom, his pickup was parked by the door and he was standing in front of it, cap in hand. "I'm sorry," he said. "Really sorry. That was so stupid, and I didn't even mean it. I didn't. Running my mouth . . . Vinnie's right about me. I'm a *cabrón*."

She didn't look at him. Didn't know what to say.

"Let me drive you back to Rita's. You fix up and I'll check out the casino, take a look around Brawley. I got his pic. I already checked RV lots. They said nobody like him bought a trailer lately. Bad economy helps. Almost no sales. So probably a motel like you said. Probably won't hook up with another woman this fast, right?"

Angel didn't trust herself to speak. If she cried again in front of him . . .

"Get in. Please. I'll be right."

Angel did, staring out her window on the drive to Rita's. This would be okay. She could get herself together before Rita and the kids got home, and she could get the pistol from the bathroom. She'd have time to look for the bullets. She'd need them sooner or later.

She left the truck without having spoken and was frustrated when she reached the front door to find it locked. Behind her, Momo was waiting to see that she was safe. She walked around the house. The rear door, which Scotty had broken, still wasn't fixed. She missed the new cigarette butt on the ground next to the doormat. Inside, she blinked the porch light once to let Momo know she was in and okay. When he drove away, she went to the bathroom to clean off the rest of the blood and change clothes.

Looking at herself in the mirror, she was ashamed. Dirty, bloody, tear-streaked face. A crazy girl. What was the matter with her? Her moods way up, way down. And opening the door of a moving truck? Was that the way she wanted to go? That reminded her. The bullets.

She checked to see that the pistol was still hidden behind the towels before entering the bedroom to search the night table on Vincente's side. A bottle of aspirin, a pack of Kleenex, a cheap watch, condoms. She felt slimy, spying on them after they'd been so good to her. The bullets were in the back of Vincente's top dresser drawer, behind his briefs and socks. Two boxes: .38 cal. and .22. She took the bigger ones.

Back in the bathroom she tried to stash them in her small purse with the pistol but it took too much space. She fiddled with the gun until the cylinder opened, fed six cartridges in the empty chambers, clicked the cylinder back in place, and hid the box with the remaining shells in the spot behind the towels. Now the pistol fit, but she noticed how heavy it felt. Would the cheap purse hold it without seams breaking? Was there another way to carry it? Where had she left her stuff with the extra clothes and green water bottle?

She finished cleaning the scrapes on her hands and knees, stuffed the torn cargo pants in the garbage, and set the blood-stained top in the tub to soak. The phone! She found it in the thrown-away cargo pants. The cover was cracked and the screen was dark. Maybe it had turned off when she fell. She pushed the red button and it stirred to life.

As she put on the clothes she'd arrived in, her old T-shirt and Carmen's baggy green jeans, she immediately thought about Momo. *I look stupid.* Was that what . . . was that why she was acting so dumb? Man-hungry like her mom? She stood through another wave of fury. She didn't want him, didn't need him . . . She could feel tears welling again and that made her even madder. Hurting herself over a guy? An older guy who wasn't interested? She stopped herself from hitting the mirror. Rita didn't need more damage.

Okay, a promise. She'd swear. From now on she'd turn off her feelings. All the way off so she could take care of business. Shoot Scotty or shoot herself. That was going to happen. She'd make it happen. And nobody and nothing would get in her way. After that? Who cared?

The older man with the gray stubble beard had walked away from the house a few minutes earlier after getting a single picture of Angel through a back window. It had to be the girl his friend wanted, and one picture would be enough to confirm it. He'd been smoking so many years he didn't give a thought to the butts he dropped wherever he went. His Suburban's floor was full of them.

22

Rita came home and sent Jessie to her room to play. "Listen up," she said to Angel, who was again looking at classifieds.

"Trailers are more expensive than I even thought," Angel said, shutting the paper.

"How come you changed clothes?" Rita asked.

Angel couldn't believe how observant the woman was. Must be the teaching thing. Her own mom had barely noticed her all these years. "Um . . ." She glanced around but couldn't come up with an acceptable excuse. "I wrecked your things. I'm sorry. I'll pay you back."

Rita just looked at her. "I got plenty of clothes," she said. "How'd you wreck them?"

"I fell out of Momo's truck."

Rita looked away. "Fell . . ." she said.

Angel didn't want to explain. It was too dumb, too embarrassing.

"I can't have you and Momo staying here together," Rita said. "I don't have enough room."

"You don't have to worry about me and Momo." Angel didn't look up. "He thinks I'm a baby. Anyway, I got where I'm staying figured out," Angel said. "I just need to borrow an extra school key for a few days."

Rita looked at her closely. Thought a moment. "The attic? You take one of the extra keys?"

Angel nodded.

"You don't think that puts the children in danger?"

Angel hadn't thought about that. She could add *selfish* to *baby*. "Scotty won't mess with the school." She considered whether that was true. "Um, messing with kids and a school would bring everybody—cops, parents, everybody—down on his head. He'd never want that kind of . . . what do you call it?"

Rita wasn't sure. "Exposure?"

Angel nodded, watching Rita think it over.

"Nope," Rita concluded. "Can't risk it. Please put the key back tomorrow."

Angel's anger flashed, but she kept silent. Maybe a part of her knew Rita was right. No. Rita *was* right. But if not the school, where? Angel pictured the blocks in Rita's neighborhood. She didn't want to be just anywhere. She wanted shelter, some kind of lookout so she could see Scotty coming. She remembered thinking about this before, like if she were up on the platform, how she'd have to watch car and foot traffic coming in from the highway, but she couldn't stay up there in the sun on that edge for long. Too uncomfortable. And probably too visible in the daylight. Scotty or anybody could see her and wonder what she was doing. And Vincente was so mad at her, his truck was no longer an option.

"What about the blue house?" Rita asked, once again thinking along with Angel. "Right at the corner of this block. That old jeep in front of it, up on blocks."

"I saw it," Angel said.

"That was the Flores place." Rita sat across from Angel, slipped off her work shoes, flexed her feet. "They moved a few months ago and they couldn't sell it, so they just left it like the jeep. Probably still has some furniture. Unless people broke in the back, it's in decent shape. Best thing? It's right on the only street in from the highway. Day or night, you could see every car."

Angel liked the idea immediately. "What if he hiked in?"

"He could always do that. Slink around. We all have to watch out for that. But if he set up and kept an eye on this house," Rita said, gesturing with her eyes around her living room, "he'd see pretty soon that you weren't here, and he wouldn't know where you'd gone."

"So you and the kids would be in danger."

"True, but if you're right, he's taken his shot here. No gain in messing with me again. He'd have to kill me or kidnap me, and everybody would know within a day. Big-time trouble."

But Angel didn't hear the last part. She was looking out the front window, watching Norma walk down the sidewalk. "Just a sec," she told Rita as she got up and went outside.

"Hi. What you doing?"

Norma smiled. "You know," she said.

"Nope," Angel said, shaking her head. "You going to the store? Getting some exercise?"

"I'm looking for him," Norma said, in a loud whisper. "Bad bad."

Uh-oh. "You can't do that."

"Yeah. You said."

Angel realized Rita was standing behind her, watching from the front door. She wouldn't like this at all. "Okay," Angel said, so softly she didn't think Rita could hear. "But you got to promise me something."

"Sure," Norma said, beaming.

"You got to only do it a little while each day. You don't miss school, you don't miss dinner or anything at home."

"Sure," Norma said.

"And one more thing."

Norma waited.

"It's a secret, right? A true secret. You and me, we don't tell. Nobody, right?"

"How come you don't want teacher to know?" Norma said, peering at Rita over Angel's shoulder.

" 'Cause it's a secret. I just told you. Right? Nobody?"

"Deal," Norma said, bumping her elbow against Angel's arm. Norma put her finger to her lips. "Nobody." She glanced over at Rita. "Hi," she said.

Rita came out to them. "What you two whispering about?" she asked Norma.

"Nothing," Norma said.

"We were just talking about games," Angel said. "Norma's really good at games and she's helping me."

Rita raised her eyebrows. She didn't buy it.

"Go on," Angel said to Norma. She gave the girl a quick hug and propelled her on her way. "See you at school tomorrow."

Norma kept walking but turned her head to look at Rita and Angel. "Bad bad," she said, and pointed to her head.

"What does she mean?" Rita asked.

"Uh, I told her she's cool, like bad, you know."

Rita snorted, gave up trying to get the truth. "Let's finish our conversation."

They took either end of the couch. "Now you're trying to try to find Scotty before he finds you," Rita said, letting Angel off the hook. "Unlikely, but let's say you and Momo luck out and run him down. Then what?"

Angel couldn't tell her. She really liked Rita but she couldn't trust her with this. Rita would try to stop her. "I tell the police, tell TJ or somebody where he is. Maybe by then they'll have found Mom. And when they arrest Scotty they'll keep him this time. Put him away. It'll be over." Angel raised her shoulders. "After that maybe I can stay somewhere around here." Angel thought Rita might like that, thought that idea might derail her from asking again about what would happen if she found Scotty.

Rita reached out and took one of Angel's hands in both of

hers. "Look at me. I think I understand how alone you feel with this problem. And I understand how when other people get involved it gets worse for you."

Rita stopped and chewed her lip.

Angel could see Rita had more to say, but she didn't want to hear it. Rita was right. Other people made it much worse.

"I respect that," Rita continued, "but lately you've started to lie to me all the time. All the time. I know you think you have to, but I've got my marriage and my kids on the line. I can't have you lying to me. Makes the risk way too high. If you can't tell me the truth . . . you have to leave."

"I WANT TO LEAVE!" Angel was up and yelling. "You think I don't want to take off? I could, too. And he'd never find me. I could walk to . . . way away and he'd never find me in a million years. You trapped me!"

Angel was scaring herself. She was out of control like the way she felt sometimes when her mom and Scotty would have those horrible fights. She needed to run. She wanted to run. She always ran. So why was she standing here? It wouldn't do any good. And it wouldn't do any good to cry. Nothing would do any good until Scotty got her or she got him. Now how do you tell that to someone you . . . to someone you . . . Angel sank back to the couch. Out of words. Out of energy.

Rita, having remained seated through the tirade, took a deep breath and finger-combed the tangles in her hair. "We can't keep doing this," she said. She didn't move closer to Angel, didn't reach out, but her face and her voice were kind. "We're at one of the hardest places people ever get to when they care for each other. Either tell me the truth, or you can't stay here any longer. Either trust me, or you have to leave and pray you can save yourself."

Rita shifted position but held Angel's eyes. "You've been taking care of yourself by yourself, pretty much since you were a little girl. You had to, and you made it work. But right now there's another step to take. Let me in. Yeah, you could be hurt. You been hurt. Do it because . . . because I . . ." Rita looked like she wanted to say more, but she stopped, put her hands in her lap. Waited.

Angel's hands and knee were burning. She should put some iodine—"I've got . . . I took—" Angel looked away from Rita. She couldn't do it. The gun was her only chance. The only real solution. "I got to go" was all she could come up with. She was trying to read Rita's face but she couldn't. "I'll stay close. I'll come to school whenever I can, but I have to hide now, until I can get out of here."

Angel scanned the living room. Was there anything she really needed to take besides the purse with the gun? "I'll stay in one of these empty houses, the one with the jeep, like you said. You're right about the attic. If Scotty gets me, I can't have kids around. I'm figuring a way . . . I'll deal with this."

Angel stood, wanted to hug Rita but didn't move forward, afraid she might cry. She hefted the purse and clasped it in front of her. "Thanks. Thanks for everything. I'm sorry. I know you don't want . . ." She struggled, but couldn't finish the sentence.

Rita stayed quiet, looking first at Angel's eyes and then

down to the purse. Rita's boy came into the living room and asked about dinner. She held up five fingers and he went away. The stillness felt heavy to Angel, but she endured it, reluctant to walk away.

"Is it loaded?" Rita asked.

Though she hoped her face didn't show it, Angel was stunned. How? How could Rita know? "What? What are you . . ." but she gave up. After an uncomfortable minute or so, Angel nodded.

"Is the safety on?" Rita asked.

Angel didn't know. She took the gun out of the purse and looked at it. Wasn't the safety what kept it from firing if you didn't want it to? There was the lever that made the cylinder open. She didn't see a safety catch.

"Do you know enough about the gun to operate it?" Rita asked.

"I fired one like it."

"Once?"

Angel nodded.

"Keep your finger off the trigger," Rita said.

"What do you mean?"

"That's the only safety. Don't touch the trigger until the very end."

23

The lock was corroded, the mechanism stiff, and Angel was afraid she might break the key Rita had given her. After several tries and some jiggling, it finally turned and the door creaked open. The Flores place was vacant but not empty and not ruined. Rita was right. From the dusty picture window in the front room you could see the whole main road into town all the way up to the StopShop. The two corner windows gave her a ninety-degree view of the intersection with Rita's street and she could see the highway north of the store from the front bedroom. Scotty would have to leave his truck, sneak around the town's borders, and come in from the seaside to surprise her.

She checked the back door, the back windows, and made a tour of each room to make sure everything was locked. Okay.

He couldn't sneak up on her unless she was asleep. Since she didn't think he'd come right away, she had a couple of days to figure out how to handle dozing off. A couple of days to decide whether to really make a run for it.

The boats she'd seen on her walks along the shore were rotted and useless and the sea was way too wide to swim, so she couldn't go east. Brawley, which was probably where he was staying, was miles south, so she couldn't see how to make that work. North, even farther away, were a bunch of towns like Thousand Palms and Desert Hot Springs, but Scotty knew that area better than she did. Straight out front, west, she'd have the Anza-Borrego badlands. She couldn't make it through that to San Diego. And if she hitched? Pretty risky. If Scotty saw her, she'd disappear forever.

So, first thing, she was here. Here. At least for the next couple of days. She could sleep on the couch, which must have been too big for the Flores family to take with them. She could eat lunch at the school, help a little with the kids, and stay out of Rita's hair.

By sundown Angel was sprawled on the fuzzy sofa, watching the road, and munching on the tortillas and cheese Rita had sent with her. Her plastic liter bottle of water and the phone sat beside her on the floor. As a hideout this was good enough. Like she'd expected, cars were few and far between. She didn't realize she was so tired.

. . . *At night, the amusement park had great colors, the brightest neon and flashing lights outlining the shapes of rides. She was up in the sky, everything laid out below her, and then she was passing through the front gate in a crowd of people headed to the double roller coaster. She had seen this place several times from the freeway and always wanted to go there . . . but now the nearby roller coaster was creaking, so maybe it wasn't safe. Maybe it was going to break and—*

Angel's eyes popped open. Noise. Creaking. Wood groaning . . . the door frame . . . She reached to the floor for the purse but couldn't find it. When she leaned over, there was enough light to see, but it wasn't there. Just the phone and water bottle. She grabbed the phone, twisted it open, but the screen was dark again and she couldn't get a dial tone.

"Angel!" A bang on the door rattled the windows.

She jumped and hoped she hadn't yelled. The kitchen. She'd set the purse by the sink while she tested whether the water worked.

"Angel!" The doorknob shook. "Hey, it's Momo."

My god, he really is going to get himself killed.

"Wait a sec," she said, struggling to remember how to get the front door open. A deadbolt. Had she locked it with a key? No, there was a small knob and a little button thing on the door. She glanced out the window to see if there was anyone else in the street, anyone else watching. Another noise froze her again. A whine? Was Scotty twisting Momo's arm? Hurting him so he would talk and get Angel to open the door?

"Easy, easy." Momo's voice.

What if she ran for the purse and he shot Momo? She couldn't live with that. She had to open the door. She made herself undo the catches and pull, braced herself for a punch or a shot. But she had trouble making sense of what she saw. Momo. Bent over. Holding a cord in one hand and petting a dog with the other. She stepped back and the dog tugged the young man inside.

Momo was too busy with the animal to notice Angel yet, so she, too, focused on the dog. Light brown coat with a white horseshoe shape under its neck. A little over two feet tall with chest maybe twice as thick as its hips. Long, curved tail that swung and bounced. Big dark eyes and a thick pink tongue sliding out of its mouth, making a dopey grin. Excited, but quiet. Angel hadn't been around many dogs, but no barking seemed unusual.

"Uh, I brought this for you," Momo was saying. "He's yours, you want him."

Want a dog? Angel couldn't even feed herself, let alone take care of a dog. What was he thinking? Was he just plain dumb?

Momo hadn't stopped talking. ". . . so he's a little injured. Sore, but he's getting better. Right side, shoulder, and uh, I guess you call it the elbow, kind of skinned up. I think maybe he fell off one of the work trucks on the highway. No collar or tag. Nobody stopped or was looking. I didn't see any signs on the road or posted at the store. He's real good. I think he'll get used to you quick. He already likes me and I got you a pack of baloney. I bet you feed him, he's yours. And you can name him . . . I been calling him 'Guy' and he comes right up and he's real stro—"

"Whoa!" Angel said it loud enough to penetrate Momo's

enthusiasm. "What am I supposed to do with a . . ." but she got it before she reached the end of the question. "Guard dog?"

"You bet," Momo said, practically breathless. "They're great! They use guys like him to watchdog those huge microwave towers you see around here. They're sweet as can be until you try to mess with their home or their master. Then it's back off or get bit, and this kind don't never let go."

"Isn't it a girl?"

"Whatever."

THE DOG, Angel named her Xena, settled down as soon as Momo left. Angel opened the pack of baloney and the dog swallowed it in one gulp and promptly went to sleep. In the morning, Angel saw that sometime during the night Xena had joined her on the couch and was now sleeping across her feet.

From yesterday's exploration Angel knew the lights and water had been turned off. To pee, she'd been using the toilet even though it wouldn't flush. She washed her mouth out from the bottle and poured Xena a drink in a bowl she'd found in the kitchen. She'd slept in her clothes and didn't have anything to change into, so all she had to grab was the purse. She thought again about a different way to carry the gun. Did the Flores family leave anything she could use? In a bedroom she found a CD case but it wasn't big enough. In back, in what used to be the laundry room, there were a couple of old sheets on the floor. She ripped a foot-wide strip from one, wrapped the pistol in it, and wound it around her waist with the gun at her back like a fanny pack. A wrinkled men's dress shirt from a closet floor worked like a jacket to cover it.

She wasn't sure how the dog would react to the kids, so she left it in the fenced yard and walked the back route to school.

Momo was in front of the building sitting in his truck when she arrived. "Hey," he called to her, "I talk to you for a sec?"

She walked to the passenger side and leaned in the open window.

"We friends again?" he asked. "I want to know, 'cause this is the last day I can take you to Brawley. I got to ride up home tonight and check in with Ramón, do some chores for my folks. Got to be working again before the weekend."

Had she forgiven him? What had she been so mad about? That he didn't want her for a girlfriend? She could feel her face reddening. He was grown up and working and she was practically a child. *He must think I'm such a freak.* Like he's gonna want a . . . a what? Maybe he thought she was a tramp like her mother . . . somebody who came on to every guy she sat in a truck with.

"Yeah," she said, not ready to meet his eyes. "I don't know what's the matter with me. I'm just weird. You know. Uh, the dog was really cool. Thanks."

"So you want to go to town this afternoon? There's a couple of clubs, a couple of motels you might want to scope out."

"Sure," she said. She glanced up to find him smiling. "So honk a couple of times. I'll come out, but I got to go now and help set up." She left for the school door without looking at

him again. Thinking instead that, once inside, she would figure out how to recharge the cell phone. She hoped that was its
only problem.

Intent on Momo and the cell phone, she missed the very
warning she had tried to prepare for just two days ago in her
neighborhood car survey. Another man she'd never met, stocky,
black-haired, middle-aged, was parked near the end of the
block, watching her from the driver's seat of a white commercial van that had not been there previously.

24

Momo handed her a photocopy as she climbed in the truck. "That's his license on top, feds' mug shots on the bottom."

"This from TJ?" she asked.

He nodded. "He gave it to Rita." Momo poked his thumb at the pictures. "Your guy still look like that?"

Angel was focused on the picture and trying to get comfortable again with Momo. She didn't pay attention to the white van as they drove past it and on out toward the highway, didn't see the man inside pick up a cell phone as he put his truck in gear and followed them at a distance.

"Scotty's hair's longer. Like the bottom one," Angel said, "but he would cut it or color it if he needed to. He probably won't change what he wears. Maybe keep a cap on."

"He thin like that?"

"Pretty much, but he's strong and he's quick like you wouldn't believe. He knocked a beer off the table and caught it before it hit the floor. And when he's drinking he gets mad real fast. The remote pissed him off and he kicked in the television before Mom or me could even yell."

"Hair-trigger?"

Angel didn't answer. While he turned south on the highway, she was busy searching under the pickup seat.

"What you doing?" Momo gave her a quick glance and reached down and pulled the lever, slid the seat back so she'd have an easier time looking.

"I shouldn't be like this," Angel said, on her knees now, peering underneath. "You got a hat or anything? Sweatshirt?" She glanced up and caught him looking down her top. Blushed. Ignored it and bent lower to cut off his view.

"You want a get-up? Fool him?"

"I can't let him know I'm looking. He sees me and I'm not sure what he'd do . . . even with you there."

"Yeah, but I can't take you in places looking funny. You gotta blend or my story don't make sense."

He was right. Angel stopped burrowing and crawled into the seat again. "So how can I change?"

Their conversation was interrupted the first time by the glitzy Red Desert Casino a few miles south of Salt Shores. Angel thought it was too close and looked too expensive for Scotty, but maybe it would be a good place to meet women. The parking lot was full of the kind of trucks he might buy.

They parked by the front door and watched the customers enter. Older people mostly, smokers, several pale like they never got outside, and some beefy trucker types. The women, at least during the afternoon, were too fat or too worn out, sadly unattractive. Angel and Momo decided to give it another look when they came back by that evening.

Next, a few miles south, they checked the tiny town that materialized out of the desert, Westmorland. It couldn't hold more than a couple thousand people. Probably too small and exposed for Scotty to choose it. There were two good-looking motels right on the highway, pickups in each parking lot. Again they decided to give it a closer look on the way back home. In the late afternoon they could watch people leave the motel rooms and head out to dinner.

BRAWLEY'S BUSINESS DISTRICT was a long straight street with fast food and chain stores at the west end. Maybe a half mile down they passed a big grassy plaza with red-tile-roofed buildings and, shortly after, the commercial center, a block-long stucco arcade full of shops and small businesses. Auto repair and service storefronts stretched beyond them to the east.

Sociedad Thrift Store was on this Main Street, near the middle, across from the Celebration Outreach Church. It didn't look open, but the door pushed easily. They didn't have any lights on. The large cluttered room was dimly lit by sunlight through the front windows. Probably helped sales. If the clerk thought anything strange was going on, she didn't let it show in her face. Angel left wearing a short brown shaggy wig, a long-sleeved T-shirt, and a ratty denim vest that made her look almost like a boy. A fake-leather tote bag hung at her side by a shoulder strap. She had to clamp it with her elbow to keep the gun from banging her hip.

When they drove off, the man in the commercial van got on his phone again before turning and heading back north where he'd come from.

ANGEL AND MOMO CRUISED THE PARKING lots at the Brawley Gardens and the Travel Palms looking for big pickups with dealer paper on the windows or remnants of advertising paint on the windshields. Nothing. They drove through lots at fast-food joints and pizza places while Angel stared through the plate glass windows.

Midway along the downtown stucco storefronts, they saw their first bar, Rosie's. Momo parked and, when the sidewalks were empty, they went in. A tall, heavy woman stood behind the bar washing glasses, shaking the water off, and setting them on the counter to dry. No customers on the stools, a couple of old guys at a side table. When they got close Angel could see the woman was wearing a ton of makeup, cakeface, and had dyed her hair an unrealistic gold.

"Want someding stronger dan seltzer, I need ta I.D.," the woman said, drying her hands on her pants.

Russian? German? Angel had no idea.

"No, hey, I'm just looking for my buddy," Momo said, handing her the photocopy. "Job opened up at the plant if I can find him."

The woman didn't take the sheet of paper, gave the pictures a look. "Dey give da convicts now a job?" she asked, flat expression.

"No. No, this is the only picture I got is all."

The woman shook her head. Began washing more glasses.

"What they want, honey?" This from the thin, wrinkled old man with a feed-store cap and a striped uniform shirt like a mechanic might wear. His buddy at the table craned around to make eye contact. "I might know him," he said. "What's his name?"

"Scotty," Angel said.

"You're cute." The wrinkled man was bracing himself to stand. "Come over here and lemme get a look at you."

"Siddown, Rudy." The gold-haired woman had both hands on the counter, scowling. "You don know nobody. An' you two, ged out," she said.

THE SECOND BAR THEY ENTERED, the Imperial Club, was dimly lit and they paused just inside the door while their eyes adjusted. Angel was startled by a loud crack and rattle.

"Dice cup," Momo whispered. "I been here. They don't never check I.D."

Angel had been wondering how old Momo was. She guessed that put him at nineteen or twenty. "We're not going to get anything, right?" she asked. Men had tried to get her drunk before. After what happened the first time, she was wary.

"No way." Momo smiled. "Just be cool."

She followed him to the polished wooden bar, where a

couple sat talking to each other and two men in straw hats sat a stool apart. The bartender, a slender man with a closely trimmed beard and tight black snap-button shirt, turned to face them, frowning as he studied Angel.

"Hey, I think I got a job for a buddy of mine, if I can find him," Momo said, stepping up to the rail.

The man put a napkin out.

"Coke," Momo said, laying the photo sheet flat next to it. "My sister don't want nothing."

The man scooped ice into a short glass and filled it with brown soda from the bar hose. Set it on the napkin and made a sign with two fingers.

Momo got the money from his wallet. "You seen him?"

The bartender sighed. "I don't see anybody."

"Hey, I know," Momo said, "but a job's pretty hard to come by. He's ready to move here. San Diego costs too much."

The man casually looked from side to side, to see whether anybody was paying attention. The couple were focused on each other and the nearest man was facing away toward the end of the bar, watching TV news. Satisfied, the bartender picked up the sheet. "I wouldn't leave San Diego for this dump," he said.

"Yeah, well, job hunting." After taking a long pull, Momo offered the Coke to Angel.

She wanted to try it but shook her head.

"So you seen him."

"Guys like this usually looking for something besides work."

"He likes the ladies." Momo smiled like what-you-gonna-do? The bartender remained silent.

"Yeah, well, thanks. We'll keep looking."

The bartender turned away to serve the woman holding up her empty glass.

Momo picked up the picture sheet and left with Angel.

Back in the truck, he was excited. "I think the guy's seen him. He called it right about looking for women."

"Maybe," Angel said, "but that probably fits a lot of guys. What do you do when you go in there?"

"Have a couple of beers after work. Some weekends when I stay down here. I got a buddy who works same shifts as me."

"You pick up girls?"

This time Momo was careful about his answer. "Uh-uh," he said. "We're just relaxing. Women in here are older. Regulars, like."

Angel watched him to see if he was telling the truth.

A knock on the pickup window startled both of them. A scrawny kid with bad teeth and a dirty green T-shirt that said KICK TRICKS stood on the curb looking in.

Momo turned the key and powered the window down.

"Saw you leave," the kid said. "Buy me a forty, I give you money?"

Angel didn't understand.

"I probably can't," Momo said. "This place won't sell out-the-door stuff in the daytime. Could get you some smoke, you do us a favor."

The kid looked at him. Waited.

"An eighth if you help us find this guy," he said, reaching over Angel to show Scotty's picture.

The boy took the picture. Studied it. "Who's he?"

Neither Angel nor Momo responded.

"Where is he?" The kid handed the picture back through the window. "What I gotta do?"

"You check all over town. Any place a guy might hang." Momo gave the boy his cell number. "Call me or meet us back here at five. You find him, see what he's driving, the bag's yours. You don't, you get to roll one."

"Deal," the kid said. "Got a copy?"

Momo handed over a folded one from his shirt pocket, and the kid skated away.

"Why'd you do that?" Angel asked.

"More eyes," Momo said, starting the truck.

"You can't be carrying dope with all the highway stops!" Angel said. Driving to Brawley she had seen traffic stalled, cars lined up on the northbound lane while green-uniformed agents with dogs searched each vehicle for drugs.

"Naw, I don't hold it, but we got some where I stay. On the road to El Centro. We'll go pick up a little bit, see if there's any place else around there worth looking at."

25

The traffic was heavy on the two-lane in each direction, the highway bordered by irrigated fields with occasional abandoned vegetable stands. No businesses, no motels. In the distance, maybe a mile ahead, Angel could see tall metal stacks and white steam rising.

"That's the sugar plant," Momo said, "and this is my place." He turned right on a sandy dirt road toward a clump of stunted trees mixed among four or five trailers. "Company rents these cheap," he explained. "Four of us to a box and do our own cooking. I can make truck payments and still give money to the family."

He pulled to a stop and waited for the pickup's dust cloud to settle. "You wait here," he told Angel. "Not sure who's home and who's dressed."

* * *

THEY SPENT the rest of the afternoon exploring nearby towns like Calipatria, which had a fancy hotel twelve miles from Brawley but was probably too expensive and a little too far away from Salt Shores. They went northeast as far as Niland, where the land east of them gave way to the bleakest of deserts.

"Place called the Slabs over there a few miles," Momo said, pointing toward the desolation. "A whole town of squatters, cardboard shacks, mobile homes. Weird place. He could stay there but I'm pretty sure he wouldn't. Too far away."

Driving, they could see for miles as they wound along deteriorating pavement on skinny back roads between irrigated fields. They crossed a couple of muddy ditches that signs called rivers. Passed clusters of trailers, or strings of shacky apartments. Puny settlements set between the two-lane and the fields that housed migrant workers. Angel checked the trucks but didn't see anything that seemed shiny or recently bought. The whole area was nearly treeless, flat, almost empty, and there were few places not instantly visible.

Back in Brawley they took a right on D Street and angled toward the city center. Off a side street a couple of blocks in, Angel spotted a cluster of pickups and motorcycles parked in front of a square cinder-block building. When she pointed it out to Momo, he frowned.

"I'm not sure about that place," he said, turning and slowing to look it over. It was dark gray with BAR stenciled above the metal door in orange letters. The glass brick window might have let light penetrate but you couldn't see through it.

"Maybe we could just check it quick," Angel said. "Scotty's kind of place, like, off the main drag."

"Stay behind me till I see what's going on," Momo told her.

Inside was almost dark and they walked past the small pay phone cubby and stopped until their eyes adjusted. After a moment she felt him reach back and grip her arm. "Sleeves," he whispered.

Angel didn't know what he meant but didn't ask. She was distracted by the ten or twelve men she could now see who had turned to face them, most with shaved heads, tattooed arms, beater T-shirts. A half dozen sat on tall stools along a bar back-lit by a hazy yellow glow seeping through rows of bottles. The others had stopped what they were doing around a pool table in the corner to her right. No one spoke.

Momo hesitated.

Angel reflexively reached for his hand, began slowly backing up.

"You see the sign?"

Angel couldn't tell who said that. She was squinting from bar to pool table, looking for Scotty.

"Says we don't serve border monkeys." A stocky man with a huge belt buckle stood and walked toward them.

"Yeah, well, we don—"

The man threw his beer mug and hit Momo in the chest before he could finish his sentence. Picked up a chair as he continued toward them.

Now Momo was backing up, sliding his feet, trying not to step on Angel and trip her. "Hey! We don't want no trouble."

177

The pain made his voice tight. He held his chest with one hand and Angel's arm with the other as he edged toward the entrance.

Angel was checking behind them, making sure the path to the door was clear.

The man with the chair drew even with them, reached past Momo, and grabbed for her free arm.

Angel evaded his move and kicked him in the shin.

The man swore and raised the chair but Momo had turned and was pulling her to the door, banging it open, stumbling into the sunlight.

They scurried down the sidewalk, blinded by the brightness, and ducked into a neighboring portico where Momo continued to drag Angel with him, opening the glass door to an office and shoving her inside. She watched him as he returned to the edge of the entranceway and sneaked a look back toward the bar. After a moment he rejoined her, his face a mix of relief and pain.

The sound of a guy clearing his voice startled them and they wheeled to see a gray-haired man sitting at a desk, holding a phone away from his ear, call interrupted. "You in a hurry for car insurance?" he asked them.

They shook their heads and left, sprinting for the truck.

"What was that about?" Angel asked, once they were back on Main.

"Some Anglos . . . we're real close to the Mexican border here. They got a bad attitude. Guess that was one of their bars. Most places aren't like that."

He drove a few blocks to the Brawley central plaza, took a left, and made a sharp turn into a parking space between two cars.

Angel, who had never driven a car, was amazed how he could talk, listen, steer, and work the pedals all at the same time.

When he shut off the engine, he rested his head on the steering wheel and shut his eyes. "Maybe this isn't such a good idea," he said, not looking at her.

Angel sat smelling the dust from the truck floor mixed with his sweat and the beer from the front of his shirt. She was sick of riding around. Scared to look in another bar. This wasn't going to work. Not the way she'd imagined it. Her plan felt childish, a little girl's idea. No, she'd have to stay here, stay on the streets to have any chance. She thought about Norma, hoping that Scotty was somewhere around here and not back in Salt Shores, where he was a danger to everyone she knew and liked. "Let me see your chest," she said. The words surprised her. Shocked her, really, but she needed to make something better. Wanted to make Momo's pain go away.

He shook his head.

Momo's cell rang and he looked his phone over for damage before answering. While Angel watched Momo's face, she felt in her shoulder bag for the phone TJ had given her. It was there in Rita's little purse along with the charger and her two dollars' change from the thrift store. She took it out and turned it on. It lit, slow but alive. Never had her own phone before. TJ had programmed it with his and Goot's numbers, but how did someone call her? She pushed different buttons but got no useful information. Would it ever do her any good? Momo's grimace brought her attention back, but she stayed quiet while he put the phone in his shirt pocket.

"People found the car Matteo was driving. Up in the arroyos near Joshua Tree. Sand and brush on it so it wouldn't be seen from the air."

"How'd they find it up there?"

"Scouting routes."

Angel didn't get it.

"People walk over the border. 'Bout a hunnerd miles from Mexicali to Indio. Stay east of the Salton you can sometimes miss the patrols."

"What about Matteo?" Angel asked.

"No sign," Momo said, looking away, out the windshield at the small bandstand in the center of the park. A young man sat on the steps playing a guitar. "Matteo'd never run away. He was about to graduate, become a citizen. The guy disappeared him."

Angel felt a pain in her own chest like the words knifed her. She had managed to put Matteo out of her mind and now she knew why. Tío, Abuela. They'd helped her and this was their reward.

"Who called?" she asked, thinking about Tío and Abuela.

"Ramón," Momo said. "He says to get my ass up home and stay away from this guy."

Angel nodded. She was thinking the same thing. She had to do the rest of this alone.

She handed her phone to Momo. "How do I find out my phone number?" she asked.

Momo took it, scowled. "Hey, your battery's really low. Don't you never charge this thing?"

Angel looked at him. She thought she had, just this morning.

Momo, disgusted, pressed the menu button. "Here, look." He brought up her information. "I should get your number," he said, but his phone rang again, interrupting him. While he answered, Angel looked to the bandstand, where some skinny boys in dreads had joined the guitar player and were passing a cigarette.

"Didn't find him," Momo said, reaching to start the truck.

"The skate kid?"

Momo nodded.

"Call him back."

Momo pursed his lips but did as she asked, redialed and handed Angel his phone.

"Hey, it's me. The girl," Angel said when the kid answered. "What happened?"

She nodded as she listened. "Yeah, okay, keep looking and if Nick—his name's Nick?—sees him again, tell him to call me."

She ignored Momo trying to wave her off. "Yeah, keep going, you get the eighth now," Angel said. "Where we met. Probably an hour."

Momo was trying to take the phone from her but she pushed him away.

"Take my number." Angel rechecked her own number and read it off. "Anything happens, call me." When she was done she turned to face Momo's grimace.

"Vincente's right," he practically yelled. "You're nuts and nobody can help you."

When she gave Momo's phone back, his eyes were blazing. "You got like a death wish?"

Angel didn't answer, held her hand out to him.

"No way," he said, shaking his head, face still colored with anger.

She kept her hand out, staring him in the eyes.

"I tole you, no."

"You have to go home," she said. "You've been great. Super. Really, thanks . . . but I have to stay here and look. I'll call Rita or TJ later and get a ride back."

Momo continued to shake his head, looking from one side to the other as if the corners of his truck or the trees bordering the plaza might hold a secret to reasoning with her. "Like the sheriff's your taxi? You can't . . ." he started, but gave up as he looked at her face. "Rita's going to kill me," he said, handing over the baggie of smoke. "Does she know your phone number?"

Angel nodded, stuck the baggie in her shoulder tote.

"Give it to me, too," Momo said.

Angel said the number three more times, memorizing it herself.

Momo programmed it, looked up when he was done, and noticed her hand still out. "What?"

"Picture."

"He'll find *you* first."

Angel didn't argue.

Momo gave in.

26

Angel stood under a shade tree, watching Momo take a right on Main, heading back to Rita's. She followed the truck's progress as it passed the far side of the Brawley plaza and disappeared behind commercial buildings. Weakness took her by surprise and she leaned against the tree. In the last few minutes she'd been so scared, then so clear and strong, but now her resolution drained like bathwater. She liked Momo. She had strong feelings for Rita. Why hadn't she gone with him?

Her knees gave and she sat, rubbed at her eyes. Hopeless. Defeated. She sat with that notion as it drifted away into a stillness that lost track of time until, without conscious thought, she stood and began walking toward the bandstand, where the kids were playing music and sharing a beer.

"Hey." A tall sandy-blond boy on the edge of the group broke away and came to meet her.

Angel saw how his clothes and his dreads could stand washing but she appreciated his open face and big smile. Close, she noticed freckles and straight teeth.

"Trev," he said, introducing himself. "You're new, right?" He raised an open hand to shoulder level in a question and pointed at her head with the other. "You in a play?"

Angel frowned and wondered why he was dissing her until she remembered the wig. Great. She pulled it off and stuffed it in the tote. "No," she said, "I'm looking for a guy." She held the photo sheet out.

"He your dad?"

She shook her head.

"Then you don't want to find him."

"You guys help me look?" She gestured toward the music group.

"Maybe," he said. "You want to meet everybody? What's your name?"

"Uh, Rita," Angel said, wanting to be careful but not knowing why or how.

The guy bit his bottom lip. "Really?"

A rush of anger mobilized her. "Forget it," she told him, walking away toward Main.

Trev scrambled to get in front of her. "Okay, no name."

Angel stopped, waited.

"Show 'em the picture," Trev said. "They'll tell you if they know him."

When he brought her over, some acknowledged her, looked at the picture, shook their heads. Others ignored her. She realized a couple of the six or seven people were girls, wearing blue jeans and loose sweatshirts, no makeup. She could fit in if she wanted to. She had to know. "You guys live here?"

Trev and the girl and guy near him laughed. "In the park? No," he said. "Well, I guess we've slept behind those bushes a couple times." He pointed to thick foliage surrounding a tan adobe park building. "The restrooms open daylight hours so you can clean up if you want."

"Where do you stay?" she persisted.

"Hoov with the guitar goes to Imperial College, family lives around here. Me and Manny—"

"Samantha," the near girl interrupted.

"Me and Samantha and Deke stay at the Slabs a few miles north, easy to hitch. I don't know about the rest. There's a mission. You need a bed, you could try that or come with us."

THE MISSION WAS A BLOCK OFF MAIN, behind and sponsored by Celebration Outreach Church. The entrance was off a four-lane parking lot, and Angel walked past the place on the far side and moved into a doorway so she could watch who came and went. Old people, broken people, bedraggled moms with small children, road warriors wearing blankets and packs. Nobody her age.

The stench of urine got her attention. The doorway. Clearly more often a bathroom. She checked the concrete floor but saw only decaying fast-food wrappers and crumpled napkins.

No turds. She tried the glass door and found it locked like she'd guessed. This was some office building or church building. Might even be empty. The smell drove her back into the parking lot, and she continued walking to Main and then again to the thrift store. Inside, she asked the woman if she could exchange the wig.

"No money back," the clerk said, rolling her eyes like this happened all the time.

"Trade it in for a cap?"

"Dollar more."

Angel agreed and found an oversize hipster cap that hid her hair. "You need any help?" she asked, suddenly imagining she could work here sorting clothes or cleaning and maybe even sleep in the back.

The clerk scratched a mole on her lower lip and gave Angel a slow once-over. "You steal?"

Angel hesitated.

"I thought so. You saved?"

Angel wasn't sure enough what the woman meant to answer that question either.

The woman turned her back to pick up a box of paperbacks. "Can't help you," she said, pulling a marking pen from her shirt pocket and writing prices inside the book covers.

Angel wasn't surprised. Anyway, it was time to check the skateboarder.

THE CURB WAS LINED with cars in front of the Imperial Club and Angel could hear Western music leaking from the front door. The kid, Kick something, was sitting on his board, back against the building, sizing her up.

"Better," he said, pointing to her cap. "You bring it?"

She dug the baggie out of her tote, and he wrapped it in a wrinkled handkerchief and tucked it in the back pocket of his jeans.

"So, I call you."

Angel couldn't think of anything to say. She thought about "be careful," but she didn't want to scare him and his guys now that she'd already given them the payoff. "Where can I stay around here?" was all she could come up with.

"Any place you want," he said, hopping on his board and gliding away.

She should have asked about Kick's buddy, Nick, the kid who thought he'd seen Scotty. Should have gotten Nick's cell number. But the skateboarder was already in the next block in the middle of traffic. She'd never catch him. *No!* She hadn't gotten his cell number either. She'd given away the dope and didn't have anything to show for it or anything to bargain with . . . She thought about it . . . Her body? She wouldn't do that. Her body and the gun were all she had left.

That realization left her feeling small and lonely. She decided to go back to the bandstand and check what she had in her tote. Maybe there was something she could trade for food or burger money. She felt a hand on her arm and screamed before she could stop herself.

A red-faced guy in a cowboy hat took a quick step backwards.

"Sorry, honey," he said, slurring. "Thought you might wanta join me for a drink."

Rage and fear were making her nauseated. "I'll ki—" She shut up before she talked herself into more trouble, wheeled, crossed the street right there, making traffic slow for her.

At the plaza, the bandstand was deserted. Angel dumped everything but the gun from her tote onto the plywood floor beside her. She hadn't brought the liter water bottle. Too heavy. But she had underwear, a toothbrush, a hairbrush, a map. The screwdriver? She had no idea where she'd lost it. Probably back at the Flores house. In the little purse, a wadded dollar bill and the phone charger. She looked around the platform for an electrical outlet. They must have a bunch of them for concerts, but she couldn't see any. She could probably plug the charger in at a fast-food place. Or the bus station. And that might be a place she could spend the night. She had a couple of hours of daylight left to find it.

FINALLY, AT DUSK, she gave up searching on her own and asked in a Shell station, where they let her charge her phone. No deal. No bus station in Brawley. Nearest one, El Centro, twelve to fifteen miles south. So now what? Walk back to the mission? The phone took another half hour, and it was well after dark on her way back to the mission when she got another call.

"You lookin' for somebody, right?"

"Who is this?" Angel didn't recognize the voice at all.

"I got somethin'. Gonna cost you."

"Uh, Trev?"

"Right, I'm a puke, look like a girl. Now's gonna cost you more."

"Nick?"

"He's got bucks to hear 'bout you. How much you got I don't give you up?"

"Nick, he's going to hurt—" Her phone went dark. "Hey!"

She wasn't sure how, but the call gave her the hiccups.

ANGEL CROSSED THE BLACKTOP LOT, tried the mission door, and found it locked. That possibility had never occurred to her and she lost it. Lost it completely and began kicking the door and pounding it with her fists. She knew she was yelling and sobbing like a madwoman but she was desperate. She had to get in. Had to get safe. *She had to!*

It was minutes before a wrinkled woman with crooked and missing teeth came to the glass window beside the door and shook her head. "Beat on it all night but ya ain't getting in. Wake enough people and they'll come knock ya shitless. Opens nine for breakfast." She left.

Angel crumpled to the ground but got up immediately. This doorway, too, smelled like piss.

THE BUSHES WORKED. Enough cover to hide. Angel lay next to the stucco wall near a corner, her head on the tote. Her empty stomach kept her awake for a while. At some point after, her cell phone roused her. She could still hear traffic on Main. It couldn't be too late.

"Hey." The skateboarder. "Did Nick call you?"

Angel was foggy with sleep. Couldn't formulate an answer.

"I can't find him. No text or nothing. He calls, tell him get hold a me."

He was gone again before Angel thought to ask for his number. She might not have remembered anyway. Her mind was filled with the new information. Nick thought he'd seen Scotty. And now Nick's missing.

A GUY WOKE HER THE NEXT MORNING, walking his dog, teasing and baby-talking and sending it chasing a Frisbee. She stood, sore and grimy from tossing and turning in the dirt all night. The bathroom was locked. Her cell phone said 8:50. Mission breakfast in ten minutes. And she could use the bathroom there. And maybe find the snaggletoothed woman and shoot her.

At the front door there was a short line of people, mostly older except for one young dad shepherding three little kids, all looking exhausted. Angel wondered if they had slept nearby in their car. She hoped they had a car. Memories of Rita and her family flooded in . . . Jessie so full of energy, the shy middle girl, the boy that was so polite. The school, Norma—tough, funny Norma—and the kid with the spider, Primo? But Rita . . . why couldn't her mom have been like Rita? Even for a week?

The line moved inside, down a bare hall, and through double doors into an open room like a school gym. Cots with rolled bedding were stacked against walls on either side, ten or twelve folding tables with cheap brown metal collapsible chairs occupied the middle of the room, and against the back wall was a counter from which two women served breakfast plates.

Angel sat with the young man and his family. He looked depressed and the children seemed barely awake. They ate slowly while she wolfed the dry scrambled eggs, fried lunchmeat, and slice of white bread. She looked to see if there were seconds, but the serving women were gone. In front of an open door that could have been a staff office, Angel saw Snaggletooth talking with a severe-looking woman in dark jacket and slacks. Both were staring in her direction. She picked up the tote and left as they were starting toward her.

A PICNIC TABLE in the plaza made a good place to watch for Scotty while she planned. If he was in Brawley like she thought, he'd probably drive along here during the day. More, she wanted to find the skateboard kid again and see if he'd talked with Nick. She hoped Trev or his friends would come back to the park, because they could probably tell her how to get along here in town with no money for a few days. But she needed to be careful and avoid that woman in the dark suit. She looked like a social worker. For that matter, Angel also had to avoid the police. They might make her for a runaway.

The plaza was still empty this early in the morning but the bathroom was probably unlocked. She headed for it to clean up. The women's door was open and a city worker was cleaning the men's. She waited for the guy to come out. "Is there a skateboard park in town?"

"Not s'posed to ride 'em on the sidewalks," the man said.

He was thin and haggard in a green uniform, with gray stubble on his cheeks, red eyes. A drinker, Angel decided. She'd lived with several.

"Yeah, I don't have one," Angel said, "but my brother does and I need to find him."

"Too damn dangerous," the man said, wiping his mouth on his shirtsleeve.

Angel waited.

"Some of 'em used to set up in the parking lot behind the pharmacy," he said, nodding toward downtown. "Put crates together, make a mess."

She thanked him, received a scowl in return. "Can I go in for a couple of minutes before you clean the women's?" she asked.

"Already done it," he said. "Some people got work."

IN A STALL SHE TOOK OFF HER TOP and jeans and brushed off the dirt and twigs from last night. Put on the other T-shirt Rita had given her and rolled the pants up her calves to change her look. At the sink, the mirror was polished metal, poor quality, but Angel was able to see well enough to make sure her face was clean. She wet her hair and brushed the front into bangs as best she could and pulled the cap down to trap them. She turned the vest inside out and put it on. When she stepped back she could see she looked pretty different. At least she didn't think the suit woman would recognize her.

The area behind the pharmacy was empty, probably still

too early. Scouting the stucco storefronts at the center of downtown, she found a discount store across the street from the Imperial Club where she could sit by the front window and pretend to examine knickknacks and cellophane-wrapped comics while she kept an eye on the bar. Scotty, if he went there at all, probably wouldn't show up before lunch. The variety store was already packed with young mothers and children, the shelves and counters full to overflowing with tons of inexpensive clothes and home stuff. Slim chance anybody would notice or bother her there. Alternating between that and the plaza, she could keep a pretty good lookout all day.

She had been drowsy until the electric bolt shot through her. Just after noon. *Scotty.* She was pretty sure, even from that distance. He left the passenger seat of a large gold four-door and crossed the sidewalk into the Imperial with a package the size of a shoe box under his arm. The car stayed double-parked and Angel strained to see the driver. Looked like an older woman with elaborately styled hair. Didn't seem like Scotty's type. Had he gone for money in the short term? Was he playing pool boy while he waited to make his move?

Angel felt acid rolling in her stomach, felt shaky. She should shoot him. Right now. Stand outside the bar door and pull the trigger when he walked out. She should. She hugged herself to pull it together.

"Are you all right, honey?" A short, heavy Mexican-American woman was leaning over her, obviously worried.

"Yeah," Angel said. "I mean no. I, uh, my mom died and I just get like this sometimes."

"You want me to bring you some water or something?"

"Uh-uh," Angel said, glancing back toward the bar. "I just need to sit here for a minute. I'll be okay."

"Well, I'm right over behind that counter," the woman said. "You rest here as long as you need to. Tell me if I can help."

Angel nodded and resumed watching the bar door. It was like she was paralyzed. She couldn't make herself get up. Shoot him? Then shoot herself? Then run? If she screwed it up, he'd grab her. The thought of him touching her made her sick.

In a few seconds, Scotty came out minus the package, got in the car, and the woman drove away.

Angel was out the door in a second but the vehicle was already too far ahead to read the license. The car looked expensive but Angel had no idea what kind it was. *Damn it!* She was no good at this. She ran after it but the light had been green beyond her and the car had moved through, heading out the road to the mountains. She would never have caught up, but it pulled to the curb just before the next light. Scotty got out again and went into a building while the car rolled away and kept going east.

Angel stayed on the other side of the street until she came even with the place Scotty'd gone into. SoCal Gun and Loan. Behind its barred plate-glass window she could see the outlines of guitars, bicycles, statues, large vases. She and her mom had accompanied Scotty to one of these in Indio where he'd traded rattlesnake skins and gemstones for a few boxes of ammunition and a pistol-cleaning kit.

The place she was standing in front of, an old hotel that had been partially converted into an antiques mall, would make a good place to wait and watch. Inside, the bald man who oversaw the shops studied her as if certain she was there to steal something. She kept a close eye on the front of the pawnshop. Several minutes passed and the warm early afternoon sun through the street windows was putting her to sleep.

"If you're not shopping you can't be in here." The man had slipped up beside her.

"It's a store," Angel said, dulled, tired.

"Yeah, well, it's private. You got to leave." He showed her a cordless phone. "I don't think nothing about calling the cops if I need 'em," he said.

Out on the sidewalk she realized Scotty had been in there a long time. What was he doing? And where could she get out of this sun while she waited? She retraced her steps to the western edge of the building and found bushes up against the brick, but no place that she could sit inconspicuously in the shade except a barbershop next door. Right. Like she was going to let some old man cut her hair, even if she had the money. Between the hotel and the barbershop was a long asphalt parking lot with a shade tree at the back. That would have to do. From the tree she could still see the front of the shop.

She sat there for another three hours according to her cell. Could he be working there? Hadn't a pawnshop guy testified for him when the feds had him? Could that same guy own this shop, too? Angel decided to pull her cap way down over her eyes and walk by the barred window, briefly window-shop, see what Scotty was doing. When she did, he wasn't there. A very fat man sat behind a jewelry case reading a magazine, but other than him, the store was empty. What happened? Back door?

Around the corner were angled parking places, all empty. When she turned down the alley, a parking alcove immediately came into view. Room for three vehicles but only one in it, a big silver Cadillac with oversize chrome wheels. He had probably been parked back here, and that meant he must have had some deal going with this shop. Another time, this could be a good place to find him.

ANGEL THREADED HER WAY through crowded sidewalks along Main, back toward the plaza. Families laughed and teased each other beside parked cars. Women teamed up with children and girlfriends, shopping from store to store. Busy, happy, they hardly gave her a second look. Angel shared their mood. She was pleased with herself. She'd been right! Scotty was here.

Her fears returned as she neared the Imperial Club and began wondering about the package Scotty had delivered. What was he doing with the pawnshop? Maybe her guess had been wrong. Maybe he was already back in business. Were there other guesses she'd been wrong about? Would he take her right away? She didn't think so, but it looked like he'd found a woman quicker than she'd estimated. She ignored the doubts. What difference did it make now? She was so close. He was practically in her sights.

Preoccupied, she was unaware that the observer had become the observed. A vehicle had been cruising Main Street, looking for her.

AS SHE PASSED the Imperial Club from the other side of the street she glimpsed the skateboarder sitting in the shade between parked cars and crossed to him.

"What's your name?" she asked as he looked up.

"What's the deal with that guy you gave me his picture?" the kid countered.

"He's looking for me, so I'm looking for him first."

The cruising vehicle had no place to park and didn't want to call attention by double-parking, so it rolled on until it could make a U-turn.

"I got to show you something," the boy said, pushing to his feet. "Come on." At the edge of the bar he kicked down a narrow concrete path to the alley behind the buildings and wheeled left, back toward the pawnshop.

Angel had to trot to keep up.

By the time the cruising vehicle returned to the bar, she and the boy were nowhere to be seen.

The skateboarder finally stopped after crossing a street and winding up next to the parking alcove where Angel had been a few minutes before. The fancy Caddy was still sitting there. When Angel reached him, he pointed at the corner of the building just before the alcove.

"What?"

"You see that?" the boy asked.

There was nothing to see. Dirty brick, rough blacktop, a tuft of stunted grass, broken pieces of plastic and bits of metal, empty cigarette box.

Angel didn't get it.

"Know what that is on the ground?" the boy asked, obviously upset.

Angel shook her head.

The boy used his toe to flip over the largest plastic shard, revealing a tiny dial with tinier numbers. "Nick's watch."

His words made her cold.

THEY TOOK THE ALLEY WEST all the way to the mission parking lot and crossed Main into the plaza. Angel had to use the restroom. Bad. When she'd finished, they sat on the bandstand.

"Tolan," the boy said. "Weird, huh? Guys call me 'Kicks.' I shortened it." He showed her his arm. "Kix" was inked below his elbow in broad blue-black letters. "So who is this guy? What'd he do to Nick?"

Angel didn't know what she should say. "He hurt my mom. Really hurt her. I don't know what he did to Nick."

"Hell, call the cops. You need to jam. Split." He looked at her to see how she was taking his advice and seemed to realize she'd already thought of that. He changed the subject. "What's yours?"

"Angel. Hey, is the mission the only place to spend the night?"

"You can't stay at my house. My mom'd have a cow."

"Yeah, so is there any place else?"

He shook his head.

"I wanted to call you," she said, "but I didn't have your number."

He shook his head and looked at her like she was a moron.

"Hit 'menu,'" he said.

She didn't understand.

"Where's your phone?" he asked.

When she dug it out of the tote he showed where the calls were recorded. "Anyone ever calls you, you got their number," he told her.

"Is this Nick's number?" she asked him, pointing.

Tolan nodded. "It won't work," he said, looking away. "He doesn't answer."

After a minute where they each sat with their thoughts, she asked if there was any place she could earn some money.

"Keep selling weed."

"I don't have any more."

"How old are you?"

"Seventeen."

He looked at her. Shook his head. "How old?" he asked again.

Angel didn't want to say fourteen. Changed the subject. "You keep looking? Call me if you see him?"

"Your guy?" he said. "From a distance."

"Either him or Nick."

Kix snorted. "Right."

"You know Trev?" she asked.

"Yeah. He don't come in town all that often."

"Anybody else help me look?"

He bit his lip. "Like I'd give up another friend?"

ANGEL STAYED IN THE PARK until her phone said 5:00 p.m. and she thought it was time to try the mission again. She didn't trust Snaggletooth, but maybe the woman wouldn't be there. Plus, if the suit was a social worker, she might not hang around past five. Angel was hungry and didn't want to sleep in the bushes again. She decided to sneak to the edge of the mission parking lot, and if she didn't see either woman, she'd get in line.

But she didn't find those women. She found another instead. A slender, muscular black-haired woman looking over the parking lot, standing patiently on the sidewalk in front of the mission door.

Rita.

It had been so hard, the whole thing. Angel couldn't help herself. She ran toward the woman, laughing and crying. *Snot-nosed kid.*

27

Rita heard her coming, caught her, and swung her around to absorb the momentum. "I'm glad to see you, too."

Angel was beside herself. "I'm sorry. I don't mean . . . I don't want—" She couldn't think of anything to say to make it right.

Rita held her tight. Didn't speak. Didn't let go until Angel settled. "I want to hear how it's going, but not here. Let's go home."

Angel allowed herself to be led to Rita's old Toyota. In the car, Rita turned to face her. "We have to deal with your bag."

Angel didn't understand.

"You still carrying?"

Angel looked around to see if anyone was watching. Satisfied, she took the pistol out of the tote.

Rita handed her a paper towel that she'd dampened with something. "Wipe it off, really well."

When Angel was finished, Rita took the gun and stuck it in the back of her jeans, pulled her shirt over it. "Good thing we don't have to drive too far." She scooched around to get a little more comfortable before turning to Angel again. "You still got the dope?"

Angel raised her eyebrows pretending she didn't know what Rita was talking about.

"Momo told me before he left for home."

Angel could feel her face coloring. "I didn't want to get him in trouble."

Rita kept looking at her.

"No. I gave it to a kid to help me look for Scotty."

"You keep it in there?" Rita said, pointing to the tote.

Angel nodded.

"Throw it away."

Angel stared at her.

"The dogs. The drug stops on the way home? The dogs will smell it and we'll be in trouble. They'll search the car, find the pistol, probably arrest us both. Don't reach in it again. Just take the whole thing and toss it over there."

"I have to get my charger."

Rita frowned, handed Angel the paper towel again. It smelled like solvent. "Wipe it off good and throw everything else in that trash can."

When Angel got back in the car, Rita handed her another

damp paper towel. "Don't touch anything else until I get you some place to wash up."

RITA PULLED INTO THE GAS/CONVENIENCE mart two blocks west. When Angel returned from the restroom, Rita lifted the gas pump nozzle and both of them rubbed the end of it to kill any remaining scent.

Angel looked at Rita like she was crazy.

"You wouldn't believe those dogs," Rita said, getting back in the car. When Angel joined her, Rita extracted a thin ham sandwich and an orange from the center console. "This'll hold you till dinner."

The first part of the drive, Angel and Rita were nervous about the approaching checkpoint. Said little. Angel asked to see the motel parking lots in Westmorland. Rita nodded. Nothing caught their eye. In a few miles they encountered the line of crawling traffic. Armed men in blue uniforms let Anglos in nice cars pass right through. Rita, Hispanic, in an old Toyota, got a much closer examination.

A man led a dog on a leash all around the car, another man with a mirror on a stick checked the wheel wells and under the bumpers. Rita had to get out and open the trunk. Angel tried to ignore the perspiration tickling her neck, running down her ribs. *Let the gun stay tucked.*

The inspection probably took only a minute or two but it felt endless. By the time the lawman waved them on, Angel's hair was wet. They were silent a while more, letting the anxiousness ebb. Rita sighed and began to fill Angel in on the latest news. She said that TJ was on his way to the site of the trailer fire to check Angel's story; going up there with casts of the tire prints.

Angel told Rita she'd found Scotty. Said it looked like he was doing some business in Brawley at the pawnshop a couple of blocks past the plaza. Told her she hadn't seen what he was driving yet, or found out where he was staying.

Rita gave her a long look, said, "You're something, girl."

Was that a compliment?

When they neared the glittery casino on their left, Angel again asked Rita to make a tour of the parking area. No Scotty. She hadn't really thought there would be.

Waiting to reenter the divided highway, Rita pulled the gun out. "You know you have to return this," Rita said, handing Vincente's pistol to Angel.

The gun was heavier than she remembered.

"You can't steal from people who treat you right."

"But then I have no chance," Angel said. "Scotty'll take me and do me and I can't stop him."

"I'm working on that," Rita said.

"How?" Angel asked.

"Don't worry about where Scotty's staying," Rita told her.

"Why not?"

"You met Abuela?" Rita glanced at Angel to confirm. "She's like a *curandera*. A wise woman. She told me: '¿*Atrapar a una pantera? Hay que atar a una cabra . . . en tu hogar, no suya.*'"

Angel looked at her. *Atrapar* sounded like a trap. She

thought *hogar* was home. A *pantera?* She had no idea. Gave up. "What does that mean?" she asked.

"Basically," Rita said, "it goes: To catch a panther, tether a goat. But do it at your place, not the panther's."

Angel thought about that. Grimaced. "Make Scotty come here?" Shook her head. "That's crazy. He's already coming here. He might already be here."

"We'll see," Rita said.

Angel couldn't believe what she was thinking now . . . If you're going to die, might as well die with friends.

THE LARGE DARK GREEN PICKUP that had been cruising Main Street earlier had left its spot at the corner of the plaza and followed the Toyota at a distance, stopping well back whenever they stopped. The driver watched them go through the motel parking lots in Westmorland, stayed a few cars behind when they went through the drug inspection, watched them check out the trucks in the huge casino blacktop area. Kept an even greater distance when they turned off the highway onto the Salt Shores entrance road, kept them in sight while Rita made the left onto her own street and let Angel out at the blue house on the corner. Watched Angel unlock the door. That was good enough. A U-turn put it back on the highway.

FIRST THING, Angel went out back to see about the dog. It was long gone. She called its name, walked out front, walked around the house. She whistled and called some more but it had clearly moved on. She knew that was only fair. She just hoped Xena found someone who would treat her well. Did most people treat dogs better than children?

Rita had told her to come for dinner and Angel went the back way, hoping she might spot the dog. No deal. She crept around the side of the house to the front, hoping she might see Momo's red pickup. No deal. She looked for Vincente's truck but didn't see that either. Maybe he wasn't home yet, so she could slip the gun back without him knowing. Had Rita told him?

There was a dusty maroon crew cab across the street, looked familiar but she couldn't place it. It didn't frighten her. Maybe it belonged to another house. Once inside she remembered. Ramón.

He stood as she entered. "Angel," he said. "You look tired."

Why was he here? He had protected her, literally given her his shirt. He'd arranged her ride down here . . . and she'd repaid him by putting Momo in danger. But he didn't sound angry. Did he come here to help Vincente safeguard Rita? *Did he come here for me?*

Angel was so very glad to see him but couldn't think what to say. "Hi" and a smile was all she could muster. "I . . . I'll be right back."

She rushed to the bathroom and got the box of bullets from behind the towels, ran to Rita's bedroom, pulled the pistol out of her pocket and emptied it. She made herself slow down to stick the bullets back in their round holes in the foam packing of the cartridge box and hurriedly stuck the box in the back of Vincente's top dresser drawer. She wiped the pistol one more time using the inside of her T-shirt and took the canvas bag down from the closet. Vincente had kept the gun in a thin oily handkerchief and she wrapped the gun in it, stuffed it all in the bag, and set it back on the shelf. She heard a sound behind her and spun around. Rita. In the doorway. Rita turned and left without speaking.

Angel went to the bathroom then and stood holding on to the sink until her heart stopped pounding. She hoped she had done the right thing. She really wasn't sure. This could cost her life.

When she returned to the living room there was another surprise. Abuela. Angel didn't know what to do this time either. Abuela looked thinner than Angel remembered. And older. Deeper lines across the forehead and around the mouth. Had sorrow done this?

Angel's rush of feelings made her dizzy. Could she run before Abuela saw her? Escape the guilt? Had the old woman come to punish her for Matteo? She remembered how Abuela had washed her face after Scotty almost caught her, how she had helped Angel escape at the church. She owed this woman her life. Angel forced herself to keep walking. The closer she got, the more she wanted Abuela to hold her and make everything all right.

The old woman heard her and turned in her direction, nodded. *"Bien,"* she said.

Angel felt like she could breathe again. She stopped a couple of feet away, unsure what to say or do.

"Okay," Abuela said, holding up a finger, like "wait a

minute." "Ramón." She looked toward the kitchen. *"Ven aquí y traduzca."*

Angel could get that. Come here and translate.

Abuela extended her hand.

Angel reached for it and allowed herself to be drawn close. Yet she hardly knew this woman. *What has happened to me?*

28

Vincente arrived in time for dinner the next night, Saturday, and they all spent the evening talking through a plan. Angel convinced them that they probably had a couple more weeks before Scotty got serious. He would wait, she told them, until it would look like Angel had run away on her own. They agreed with her reasoning and decided to spring their trap right away. Goad him into action.

They would spend the weekend making the blue house as safe as possible: nailing windows shut, reinforcing doors, drilling peepholes, putting a ladder to the roof crawl space, and bulletproofing part of the attic floor with a heavy metal plate that Ramón had brought.

They would also make a hundred copies of Scotty's picture and Tuesday morning Ramón would drop them all over

Brawley with Angel's cell phone number on them. They believed Scotty would call Angel, and when he did, she would taunt him, saying she was looking for him, coming after him. That he could run but he couldn't hide. She'd say she was ready to meet him in the plaza and shoot him. Tuesday afternoon late. After the local families had gone back to their homes.

At dusk, she'd meet him at the bandstand. Angel would be there with Ramón and several of his and Rita's friends from this area. They'd be ready and waiting. But they were sure that Scotty wouldn't show. He'd know it was a trap.

What *would* he do? He'd watch. From some place near. He'd see them challenge him and laugh at him . . . and finally give up on him and go back to their homes. And he'd follow Angel back . . . to the blue house. He'd finally see where she was holing up. He wouldn't know that when Angel came home from the mock showdown, she'd hide in the attic. He wouldn't realize that Ramón and Vincente had returned to the blue house earlier and set up with their weapons.

Scotty would wait till the middle of the night, till everything was quiet, till the neighborhood was asleep, and then he'd sneak into the house. But at that point, Ramón and Vincente would either disarm him or shoot him. And then call the sheriff. They would have Scotty where they wanted him, on their own territory. And they would take care of him, for good if necessary.

The men felt certain Scotty would be provoked into responding. He wouldn't ignore that prodding and humiliation. Angel and Rita weren't so sure, but they were outvoted. The group went over every bit of it. If Scotty didn't come the first night, he'd come before long. It was definitely worth a try.

On Monday morning Angel went to school for a couple of hours to help Rita set up. She wanted to see Norma and tell her she didn't have to worry about "Bad Bad" anymore. Angel swept, set the tables for morning snack, washed and sliced the apples, put out the graham crackers.

Norma found her while she was sorting the games and putting the right pieces in the right boxes.

"That don't go there," Norma said, shaking her head like Angel was a dummy.

Angel was holding an inch-long metal race car, poised to put it in Candyland.

"That's Mopoly," Norma said, her patience obviously strained. She took the piece, opened the Monopoly lid, and stuck it inside.

"How about the rest of these?" Angel asked, pointing to a pile of fifteen or twenty pieces near the edge of the small game table.

"I'll do 'em," Norma said. "You watch. Maybe you learn something."

"Who says that to you?" Angel asked.

"Momma," Norma said. "And Momma wants to know what's wrong with the keys?"

"What keys?" Angel could never quite follow Norma's changes of conversational direction.

"School keys," Norma said. "You lose 'em?"

"Nope," Angel said, and that reminded her. She walked away for a moment to replace the attic key she'd stolen.

"Why come the locket truck been parked here?" Norma asked when she returned.

"I don't know," Angel said. "I wasn't here. What's a locket truck?"

"I own't know," Norma said. "You gots any candy?"

Angel stayed for snack time and sharing circle before she went back to help with the blue house prep. On her way out she asked Rita, "Was there a locket truck here yesterday?"

Rita was clearly puzzled. "What's a—oh, a locksmith? There was a locksmith truck out front Friday or Saturday, must have been doing something for one of the neighbors. Why? . . . Locket? That's funny," she said. "Sounds like something Norma would say."

Monday afternoon, on the walk back to the blue house, Angel remembered. Two guys testified for Scotty. A pawnshop owner and a locksmith.

THE HARDEST PART OF THE HOUSE preparation had been getting the thick metal plate up through the ceiling hole. Once Ramón and a friend of Vincente's accomplished that, the rest of the work went quickly. When everything was finished, Ramón showed Angel what he wanted her to do.

"You get back from the plaza Tuesday, you go up this ladder," he said. "We'll have a pillow and blanket, water bottle, snack. You lie right on the metal. I'll put cardboard so it don't make you cold. If there's shooting, bullets don't go through that steel. You haul the ladder up soon as you climb it and nobody but Vincente and me'll even know you're there."

"Maybe you should let the sheriff set the trap, handle him when he comes," Angel said. The closer this got, the more she was beginning to worry about someone else she cared for getting hurt. What if Scotty started shooting?

"*Policia* had him before and let him go," Ramón said. "We'll see what TJ finds, whether they go for murder. I don't know, I got a feeling this ain't gonna end till we end it."

Angel felt strange hearing someone else talking about killing Scotty. She was sure that's what Ramón meant. She guessed Ramón had a blood stake in it now with Matteo gone.

29

Alone, the blue house felt almost too quiet as Angel sat on the couch in the living room's dim light and thought about what was going to happen. What could go wrong? She didn't like the idea of the locksmith nosing around the school or around the neighborhood. What had he seen? What information had he passed on? She bet he was Scotty's friend. Could Scotty already know she was staying at the blue house? The longer she thought, the more she worried.

She jumped when her cell phone rang. Had to look for it. Without the tote, she didn't have a particular place for her things anymore . . . not that she had anything left besides the phone and the charger and some of Rita's clothes. Found it by the third ring.

At first she thought it was a wrong number. Sounded like somebody coughing or crying.

"They found Nick."

"Tolan? Uh, Kix?"

"Run over." He tried to clear his throat. "That empty area by the airport? He never goes out there."

"We can get this guy. I know where to find him," Angel said. She could make this right.

"Hell, no. Forget it. You got Ni—"

Angel could hear the catch in his voice, knew he was trying to keep it together. "Do you drive?" She needed one last bit of help.

"You got to tell me!" Yelling now. "Am I next?"

"Can you give me a ride to town?"

The phone went dead. Connection ended. She tried calling back, screamed into the receiver, but it didn't do any good. He didn't answer, couldn't hear her.

Okay. *No.* Not okay. Not ever going to be okay. She could end this. Without anybody else getting hurt. Without Ramón risking his life for her. She knew from the way he'd been talking, Ramón had brought a gun with him. She hoped it was a pistol, but anything would do. He probably wouldn't bring a weapon into Rita's. Too many kids. He'd leave it in his truck.

She stuck the phone in her pocket. Out the front door she crossed the street and used scrub brush for cover till she reached the crew cab. The doors were locked. Made sense with important stuff inside. She didn't want to break a window, walked around the rear of the vehicle looking for another idea. The back of the cab had a split window. Scotty's old truck had the same thing. When you put a camper on the back you could reach through the window to get something or you could just open the thing for ventilation when it was hot.

She climbed into the truck bed using the stock rails for leverage. Held her breath when she got to the window. It was closed, but was it locked? No! She spread the sides apart. Could she reach through far enough to unlock a back door? No. Could she climb through? This was the first time she ever remembered thinking she was glad for small boobs. She was able to scrape through the opening as far as her hips but that was it. Wiggling, she turned herself to the side and reached for the door handle, pulled it, and the lock clicked up.

She climbed down from the bed and began with the door she'd unlocked. A jacket and extra hat were on the seat. Under a blanket on the floor she found his shotgun. It was long and heavy, and she left it alone. She pulled the front door lever and opened the driver's side. Change in one of the drink cups, fast-food sacks on the passenger floor. Under the seat, a hard, heavy lump wrapped in a cotton T-shirt. Unfolded, it was a pistol. Not the kind where you could see the bullets. It was the best she could do. Lucky to have anything at all. She shook out a Burger Boy sack and stuck the gun in it. Had she used up all her luck? Maybe. She took off running across the field for the highway.

* * *

ONCE YOU NO LONGER CARED, hitching was easy. She got a ride within minutes. A flatbed driver hauling planter boxes. Said he was headed to El Centro, happy to drop her in Brawley. He looked at her more than the road but he didn't touch her. She closed her eyes to shut him out but immediately had the feeling she was falling, and it got hard to breathe. *What am I doing?*

She had to open her eyes to keep from screaming. To her right, out the passenger window, the sky was faded, empty of clouds, and rough brown ridges were stacked into one another, looking scorched like she was already in hell.

She was going to die. Today. She could feel it. And then worse . . . what if she got too scared to pull the trigger when she finally found him? What if Scotty threw her over his shoulder and carried her to his truck and started touching her? Drove her out somewhere in this barren . . . and then she'd join her mother, another body in the sand. Acid was in her throat and then her mouth and she hurriedly rolled down the window to spit.

She clutched the gun to her middle, held it tight to stop the sudden cramping. She couldn't let that happen. Not that way. She had to shoot him. What a stupid life when the most important thing you ever do is pull a trigger. And after that? She guessed she'd pull the trigger again. And that got her to thinking about never seeing Rita again. And Momo and Norma and Ramón and Abuela . . . She kept her face turned toward the window so the driver wouldn't see the tear tracks and want to talk to her.

30

The driver let her out on Main at the stoplight a block from the pawnshop where he had to turn south to El Centro. She wasn't ready to walk through the door or even look in the window. She went instead to the alcove in the alley. The Cadillac sat in its usual place, and next to it was a dark green extra-cab pickup, jacked up a little, clean, new tires. Angel knew. And the knowing made her completely hollow. She'd never had a sensation like it. No stomach, no heart. Breathing and muscle, that was all.

She would go in through the back door. She pulled out the gun and let the paper sack fall to the ground.

Angel could feel her heart drumming. She had only been sitting and walking. It seemed weird to be out of breath. In the quiet, she could pick out the noise of an air conditioner, and occasional sounds of trucks gearing down for the stoplight out front. She knelt for a moment behind the pickup bed and watched the back door. She had thought it was screened but now she could see it was some kind of safety glass that had wire all through it. Was it unlocked?

She tried to remember what she had seen a couple of days ago when she looked in the front window. A horseshoe of counters. A gross man with an enormous stomach sitting on a high stool behind the one at the back, reading. Behind the man, there had been a curtained opening probably leading to a storeroom. So behind the glass door she was watching? Probably a storage area. And then would come the curtain she'd seen connecting to the salesroom.

Remembering how the man looked, Angel guessed he sat most of the time, so where would Scotty be? Probably behind one of the counters, working on something. Stringing a necklace of teeth, taking a pistol apart, lubricating a trap, something like that. He usually kept his hands busy. Would he be armed? Probably not carrying more than his skinning knife, but there were racks of guns in arm's reach. And probably bullets in a drawer or in a case on the back wall. She would go in and surprise him. The fat man would probably drop to the floor and she would shoot Scotty before he could load a pistol. Shoot him and . . . leave? Turn the gun on herself? No, she'd run. She bet she would.

She snuck between the car and the pickup, edged along the back wall of the shop. In the afternoon sun, the light stucco burned and the aluminum door was even hotter. She got a handful of T-shirt, tried the handle, and it moved. *Unlocked. Okay. Down to this. No going back.*

Something was bothering her, niggling at her attention, something she was forgetting. The unlocked door? Was Scotty out back somewhere and she had missed him? She leaned down far enough so she could look under the cars. Didn't see feet. Maybe he went out for a couple of minutes and left it open 'cause he'd be back soon. Or maybe the elephant just forgot to lock it. Whatever it was, she couldn't remember. When she pulled the handle down, the hinge made a tiny clink and then stayed silent. She paused and, when no alarm went off, slipped inside.

THE BACK ROOM WAS DARK, its only illumination coming from the passageway to the front. Angel now saw that the entry wasn't a curtain but rather translucent plastic straps that hung from ceiling to floor. In the dimness she could make out wire baskets on cheap shelves around the walls. The wall at her left had a workbench against it, and next to that a half-open wooden door to a toilet. Angel listened but didn't hear anyone in there. Careful not to bang into anything, she stepped forward to the straps. Distorted shadows moved across the light, giving her creeps. People walking by on the street? Customers? Scotty? She pushed one strap a half inch to the side and looked through.

Snowboards and guitars, paintings and hunting bows hanging high on the walls. Shelves filled with musical instruments, boom boxes, and cameras. In spite of the glare from the front window, over the front door she could see a large hawk perched on a section of varnished post. That looked like some of Scotty's work.

The fat man was sitting on a stool behind the back counter to her right, moving his lips in and out as he concentrated on untangling necklace chains. He wheezed softly with each breath. Angel grimaced when she smelled his body odor.

She stepped to the other side of the entryway. Saw shelves of motorcycle helmets, drums, a long sawhorse of saddles and bridles. She still couldn't see Scotty. The stool creaking got her attention. The fat man leaned to the side and turned up the speed of a standing fan that swept the room. Angel leaned back, gave him a minute to get engrossed in the necklaces again, and then edged farther into the door until she could see the whole room. No Scotty. But she was sure that was his new truck in the back parking place. Okay, she would wait.

She leaned back against the doorjamb and noticed her top was soaked with sweat. Made herself ignore it. She must have zoned out for a moment, because she was hearing footsteps but hadn't heard the man get up. She lifted the gun and wheeled into the door. The fat man was bent over a couple of feet away, putting a CD in a stereo. He straightened as she faced him and pointed the pistol at his stomach. The man dropped the CD. "Don't!" he yelled. He lowered his voice, pleading. "I don't know you." A dark stain spread onto the front of his slacks.

Angel didn't want this. Didn't have a plan for this. "Where's Scotty?" was all she could think of. Angel's hand cramped and she accidentally squeezed the trigger. She yelled, surprised, but nothing happened. The pistol didn't fire. *What the?* This had happened before! What did she have to do? She pulled at the top of the gun but it was stuck. Looked at it. A lever was jammed in a notch. She thumbed the lever down, but the man reached her as she raised the pistol again and knocked it out of her hand, sending it clattering to the floor behind her. She kneed him as hard as she could under his stomach, hoping for the groin, and he stumbled back a step and doubled over. Angel didn't notice as she focused on putting her whole body into the next kick like she'd had to once with her mom's trucker friend. The man got this kick square in the nose instead of the nuts. That ruined him and he toppled into the doorway, tearing down the plastic straps as he fell.

Angel gave the counter a glance to see whether there was something to hit him with. Indian rugs, plastic sort trays of jewelry. Nothing useful. She eyed the wall rack behind her, but the rifles were locked together with a metal cable through their trigger guards.

"Hi, honey, I'm home."

Angel froze. He must have come in through the front door while she'd been busy.

"I've been thinking about you, baby, and I was right. You still look good enough to eat."

She could hear him continuing to walk toward her, but she couldn't make herself turn around. Couldn't stand to see his face. "Stop!"

"Sure, sweetie. We got a lot of time to get reacquainted."

She thought she heard him take another step.

"What did you do with Arthur?"

A moan came from the floor behind the counter.

What had he seen?

"You stab him? I'm surprised he noticed it. Hey, Arthur, you okay?"

The man groaned something.

She was pretty sure Scotty took another quiet step but she still didn't turn. "Stop! I mean it."

"Relax. You came to see me, honey. I'm just making sure you get a proper welcome."

It sounded like Scotty hadn't seen the scuffle with the fat man. Didn't know her pistol was a few feet away on the floor. Since he'd come in off the street, he probably wasn't carrying a gun. So she had to move before he got hold of her.

"I like that little butt, but how come you don't look at me? You got some burns you're hiding?"

Torching the trailer. Angel could hear by the sound of his voice that he was pretty close, and if he could see her butt behind the high counter, he was way too close.

She wheeled and he stopped maybe eight feet away. With her hands below counter level she searched for the opening to the cabinet under the glass top. She had just seen hunting knives. Big hunting knives.

Scotty put his hands on his hips. "You know, Sweet Cakes, I can't tell you how often I thought about seeing you again. And that Rita's smokin'! She lonely?"

"Don't take another step or I'll kill this guy," Angel said, making her face look hard and serious.

Now Scotty put his hands up in mock surrender. "Okay!

Okay. Jeez. Don't go mental. I'm not going to hurt you in the middle of a store." He took his eyes off her. Spotted a stool near him that customers would use. "Hey. You stay cool and I'll sit down here and we can talk."

Angel shook her head. And where was the damn catch to the cabinet? Her fingers found a round metal lump. *Locked.*

"Easy, Ainge. I'm going turtle slow here. Just sit and talk. That's all."

Angel quit shaking her head. Watched him pull the chair away from the side counter and a little closer to her. Even though the front window was tinted, him sitting with that brighter backdrop still made him a little hard to see. Okay, let him talk while she figured out what to do. "This your new business?" she asked him, scanning the room with her eyes and in the process trying to locate her pistol, see how far away it was.

"Just money, honey," Scotty said, half sitting, putting a boot on a stool rung. "You know me. Like to be outside."

Angel took a step to her left and leaned her elbows on a folded rust-colored rug. Felt slowly with her foot, hoping to touch the gun.

"You know the sad truth, baby, your mama wasn't no damn good. And she rode me like a dog. I don't know if you miss her but I don't." He waited for Angel to speak.

She tried to look like she was listening, pushed up with her hands and readjusted her position another step toward where the pistol must have wound up.

"I got something I bet a dollar you don't know," Scotty said, little smile, sincere. He nodded. "Yeah, I tried to hurt you a little."

Angel pictured the flaming trailer. *Liar!*

"And yeah, I been after you." Scotty shook his head like he couldn't believe what he was going to say next. "But truth is, I missed you." Scotty looked away like he was embarrassed. "Truth to tell, I kind of, uh, you know, like you." He looked at the floor.

Angel was having trouble concentrating on her search. *Is he nuts?* But could this buy her more time? "I, uh, I thought about you a lot, too," she said, trying to keep her face, her expression absolutely still. She turned to the side as if to think this over. When she turned back, she was another step farther and her left foot bumped metal. *Bingo.*

"Gimme a sec, here, sweetie. I mean it. You think you could maybe put this all behind us and we could get together?" He paused, studying her for a response. "I got a dynamite trailer now. Give you like fifty a week spending money. We could, you want to, go somewhere. Vegas. L.A." His voice was so reasonable, so even. Scotty at his best.

Angel tried to look behind his eyes. *He means it. He is nuts.* She could drop right now and have the gun. "How would I know you've changed?" What could she say to relax him one more notch?

"Aw, Ainge, you know people don't never really change. Sad but fact. That's why you're dicking with me."

He was off the stool, diving over the counter before she could more than straighten. He had her shoulder but missed her arm because she twisted it at the last second. When she dropped, he wound up holding half a T-shirt.

She grabbed the gun and tried to roll for some distance but he was too close, had her by the ankle. She kicked at his eyes with her free foot. He scrunched them shut, ducked his head, and pulled at her. His hand on her skin, his touch was electrocuting. What could she hit him with? Kicking and writhing, she caught a glimpse of something in the corner angle at the wall. Took a microsecond to look. A broom and, beside it, a dustpan. He made a hard tug and his face was at her waist. She lunged to reach the dustpan and threw it at his head. It caught the corner of his eye or just below it. He yelled with pain and rage and she was up, onto the counter and past him while he thrashed. The fat man was still on the ground, holding his face, moaning like a baby, when she slid down, stepped on him, and sprinted through the back door to the rear of Scotty's truck. There she rested the pistol on the corner of the tailgate, aimed at the door, and waited while she tried to regain some air in her lungs. She remembered what had been bothering her earlier. *The panther. Don't go to his place.* She was a fool but she was still breathing.

The back door opened and the fat man came out. Saw her pointing the gun. Started to raise his hands but keeled over instead, out of sight in front of the Caddy. Yelled, "Scotty!"

The back door opened again and she fired the gun, holding

it to the truck rail so it wouldn't fly out of her hand. Stucco flew off the wall as she watched Scotty duck back inside.

The fat man might have been jabbering. He might have been screaming but Angel was deaf . . . or deafened. The gun's discharge was like a bomb going off. She kept the pistol balanced on the top of the tailgate, sighting at the door. Time passed while she continued to struggle for breath. Was the fat man crawling around the vehicle? In a moment she thought she heard the car door opening, thought she heard it start, glanced to see smoke puffing out the exhaust, and then the Caddy was hurtling backward into the alley and away out of sight until there was a horrible banging crunch, a horn honking, and finally silence again.

Angel didn't have time for that. She was focused on the door. Where was he? Was he getting a machine gun? Okay. She was ready to die. She'd get off at least one more shot.

"Drop it, sweetie." From behind her. He'd gone out the front door and circled. She should have thought he might. She was no good at this. "Let it go, Ainge. Don't turn around."

But she did. And fired. And missed him. And fired again. She could see how wide his eyes were. See the huge hole in the barrel of the gun he pointed at her. But he didn't fire. And she knew once again. Right here, this was too big a mess to explain away. Murder. Cops would wise up and he'd be on their radar big-time.

He wheeled and ran as she fired again, ran full speed, ran for all he was worth toward the corner, and hit Rita like a freight train just as she came barreling around the side of the building. He never had a chance to react. Knocked her ass over teakettle, end over end across the sidewalk into the street, and in the process tripped himself. Ramón, who was a second behind Rita, hit him so hard with the shotgun that the stock splintered, and Scotty tumbled and skidded on his face till he slid unconscious off the curb into the gutter.

But Ramón wasn't done. He took in the scene. Twenty feet down the alley Angel was standing motionless, stunned, looking back at him. Swiveling the other way, he surveyed Rita for signs of injury and scanned both directions to see whether she was in danger from traffic. Deciding the two were temporarily safe, he moved quickly to the man he now knew as Scotty and turned him over. On the pavement nearby he located Scotty's pistol, pressed it into the man's limp hand, and used Scotty's finger to fire the gun into the air till it was empty. He let Scotty fall back and ran to Angel, who remained frozen at the spectacle. He yelled something at her that she didn't catch and began prying his gun from her hand. He thumbed the safety, stuck the pistol in his belt, and hurried to help Rita. All in a few seconds. A flurry of action and a story to tell the authorities that mostly left Angel out.

THE SILENCE VIBRATED FOLLOWING THE SHOTS. Angel had remained still as the echoes faded, but the sight of Ramón kneeling beside Rita moved her into a dreamlike walk up the alley.

Angel stopped as she reached Scotty. Practically deaf at the moment, she was still aware of a roaring fury that boiled inside her. This man had killed her mother. Angel stifled an impulse to kick him and thought of the gun. What had Ramón done with it? Was it empty?

Scotty stirred, opened one eye, then the other, and rolled himself partway over as he gradually came back to consciousness. He jerked when he saw Angel standing directly above him.

Angel saw his eyebrows rise as he realized she was looking at the gun he held. Saw his hand tighten on the grip as he considered shooting her. She thought he'd been unconscious when Ramón fired all the bullets. *All* the bullets? Was the pistol empty? Angel stood her ground.

Scotty braced himself to pull the trigger, kill her right now . . . remembered. Stopped. He'd been seen. He'd smashed into someone. There were other people around. He'd have to shoot everybody. No way he could kill her and get away clean. He relaxed and looked up to meet Angel's eyes. Saw the blaze. Could feel it. The little bitch would murder him.

But Angel walked away. Walked away to kneel beside some woman. Walked away like he was nothing.

IT TOOK WEEKS to sort out the whole thing and get charges clarified and start the placement proceedings. The most important difference this time, as far as Angel was concerned? Scotty was locked up without bail and not likely to get any. TJ, first with the help of the tire prints, and then with the help of a Cahuilla Indian tracker, found a thirty-four-year-old woman, Lila Lee Dailey, buried on a mountain ridge east of

Thousand Palms bordering Joshua Tree National Park. Authorities were able to link evidence found at the scene to the more recent murder of Nicholas Jared Patterson of Brawley, California. TJ was given to understand by state officials that the prosecuting D.A.s had ironclad cases.

Angel cut out and kept a part of the local news article.

Currently a ward of the state, Angela Ann Dailey was released to the temporary custody of Vincente and Rita Casanueva of Salt Shores, pending possible long-term placement with same.

But before all that got settled, there was a celebration, a picnic, and a lesson. The celebration? Ramón's wife, Carmen, had phoned Rita's Tuesday night, a day after the pawnshop shooting, more than two weeks after Angel's mother had been murdered.

Rita handed the phone to Ramón, who listened for two or three seconds and gradually sank to his knees. Rita, alarmed, pointed at Vincente, who took the phone and listened. When he hung up, he looked shaken.

"Carmen said a doctor called her last night. From Mexico, from Clinica Poblana in Mexicali," Vincente reported. "Said Matteo's hurt pretty bad but healing. Said he's been deported. Told her he was incredibly lucky to be alive and had a hell of a story. Said Matteo'd probably be able to call her himself in a few days."

The room was silent, everyone speechless. Angel herself had given up hoping when they found the car, had been carrying his death like a stone in her heart. But he wasn't dead! Abuela started the pandemonium with *"¡Bendito Dios!"* and everyone erupted with cheering and crying and prayers of thanks.

THE FOLLOWING SUNDAY, mid-morning, the group walked north along the barren Salton shoreline a quarter-mile past the club to a dry wash that occasionally emptied runoff into the sea. Vincente spread the blankets, put rocks on the edges so they wouldn't blow away. While Rita and Abuela set out food from the baskets, Ramón opened the cooler and handed sodas around. Norma had brought a leather string and was gathering barnacle shells for a necklace.

"Why don't I show you this before we eat," Ramón said, motioning for Angel to come with him. Rita looked up when Ramón tapped her on the shoulder. "You gonna join us?"

"Wouldn't miss it," she said, standing and picking up her daypack.

"Can I come?" Norma asked, already wet to her waist getting the shiniest-looking shells from the water.

"In a few years," Vincente told her. "You want to make some bracelets, too?" he asked the girl, reaching in his jeans pocket. "I brought some neat stuff back from Santa Fe."

"YOU'RE PLENTY SMART, plenty tough," Ramón told Angel as the three of them walked up the wash to a deeper cut with a high bank, "but I'm hoping you never need nothing like this again. Have no reason." He looked at her to see if she was paying attention. Glanced at Rita.

"You know why, right? You were real lucky," he said.

Angel knew that was true.

"Could have killed Rita. Right?"

Angel knew she had this coming. It made her sick to think about it. If her last shot at Scotty had hit Rita instead.

"We been talking. Vincente, too. Got to teach you and pray you never use it."

Rita set the daypack down, reached inside it, and withdrew a glossy magazine. The target. She walked over and propped it in the dirt about halfway up the bank of the gully. Came back and lifted Ramón's pistol out of the pack, then two clips of ammunition. Handed it all to Ramón.

"You ever pick up a gun again," Ramón said, "you keep your finger off the trigger till you see if it's loaded." He showed her the empty butt of the grip. "If there's a clip in there, eject it."

Angel nodded.

"You check the chamber . . ." He racked the pistol, demonstrating.

That sound, hard metal, *cha-chick*. Memories flashed. Angel hugged herself, suppressing a shiver.

LATER, FOOD HAD NEVER TASTED BETTER. Early that morning Rita had shown Angel how to prepare the cornmeal masa for tamales and Vincente had taught her his special rolled taco recipe with chorizo, eggs, white cheese, and a pinch of chili-cinnamon mix. Angel had been moved because she didn't remember anyone teaching her how to do home things except for a foster mom who had strict rules about making the bed. Angel's mom's idea of a picnic had been a bucket of chicken.

Angel sat on the blanket nearest the water, between Norma and a napping Abuela. The meal and the sun had made her sleepy too. She faded in and out, listening to gulls squawk or picking up on Rita's laughter as Vincente and Ramón teased and told stories.

Vincente tossed a pebble to get Angel's attention. Said, "Looks like you got an amigo."

"More than a friend," Angel said, giving Norma a squeeze, "she's like my little sister."

"I meant that dog," Vincente said, pointing. "He's been watching you all afternoon."

ACKNOWLEDGMENTS

I have many to thank for the creation and sustenance of *Desert Angel*. I appreciate my agent Tracey Adams, her husband Josh, and publisher Simon Boughton for making this project possible. I am honored to work with Wesley Adams, my editor, and I am grateful for the many, many ways he has enriched the quality of this manuscript.

The idea for this story arrived spontaneously on a business trip while I was cruising down a desert two-lane at dusk, looking east into the craggy ridges that border Joshua Tree National Park. The area was beautiful, desolate, and in its own way fearsome. Somehow Angel sprang to mind.

My psychotherapist wife has been involved with this book from its inception and I could not have written it without her keen eye. I also shared its weekly progress with the best writing group in the world: Kathryn Gessner, Carla Jackson, Melinda Kashuba, and Robb Lightfoot. Their perceptions and support were invaluable.

Special thanks go to Lindsay Reed for her most excellent translation consultation. I admire her outreach work with the Mexican American immigrants in the Paso Robles area. Further thanks to the Imperial County Sheriff Deputy, Salton City substation.

Dr. Paul Swinderman gave me ongoing medical consultations pertaining to the storyline. Manuel J. Garcia, attorney at law, provided similar advice and perspective in legal areas. My daughter, Jessica Rose, gave unfailing encouragement, and, as always, I benefited from the consistent inspiration of my writing community. An alphabetical THANKS to Steve and Kelly Brewer, Chris Crutcher, Jim Dowling, Tony D'Souza, and my man who lives his writing, the author of *Scratched Up*, Bill Siemer.